Run With the Hunted 5: Insert Coin to Play
By Jennifer R. Donohue

I0456987

For Jim

Run with the Hunted © 2022 by Jennifer R. Donohue

Ebook ISBN: 978-1-945548-19-2

Paperback ISBN: 978-1-945548-20-8

RUN WITH THE HUNTED 5: INSERT COIN TO PLAY 3

Chapter One

"How long should this take?" Dolly asks after her second cigarette and I shrug. Bristol's entering our team in the game while Dolly and I wait in the parking lot, Dolly sitting on the hood of the car and smoking, me drinking my first iced coffee of the day or my final iced coffee of the night. I didn't mean to not sleep, it's just how it happened.

We weren't all in the same city when I floated the idea of the game for our next job, and after we got her from the airport, I had to make sure Bristol was prepared for the entry challenge. And then we had to make sure equipment we needed was ready to be packed in the car. Could some of it have been done this morning? Yeah but I was already awake.

"I'm not worried yet." After all, Bristol could just be chatting with and charming people, entry already secured. She likes socializing, and even though she prefers to be a little snobby, she likes to be able to talk to anybody. So practice is practice.

"Okay but when will you be worried? Can you set a timer or something?" She grins at me and I laugh.

"Nobody in there is going to have a gun or anything but the casino guards," I say. "And not all of them will."

"Yeah that's true. Hey, maybe I'm lookin' at this wrong, and it's the nerds I should be concerned about. They've never talked to anybody like Bristol, she'll eat them alive."

"That might be true." Granted, a lot of people haven't talked to anybody like Bristol. It's part of how she's so effective.

While I'm not technically banned from entering this game, it seemed like a good call to let Bristol be our point of entry instead, just in case. This isn't life or death. We don't even really need the money. A lot of games like this don't even *have* a prize, but in this case, the prizes are lucrative (cash, crypto wallet) and fun (a motorcycle referencing a classic manga/anime that's so respected that there have been few remakes though many dreams, with a matching jacket) and interesting (a 20th century IBM computer chip.) And it'd be nice to have a payday where we aren't necessarily risking our lives or breaking the law.

Not that breaking the law bothers us much, obviously, or we wouldn't keep doing what we do.

Due to the nature of the setup, I didn't put a wire or camera on Bristol before she went in. She even took out her earbud. If a thing like that was discovered, she'd be accused of cheating and barred. We don't even know what the entry challenge is, beyond the roll of actual physical quarters that gets you through the door. If it's a puzzle or riddle or game or what. The challenges vary throughout the game itself, and the gamerunners aren't totally the same from year to year, adding some newer winners, dropping some past winners. Just the way these kinds of games work.

The automatic doors woosh open, and Bristol click-clacks out. I told her there might be locations in the game that she won't want to be in a dress and heels for, but she told me she'll do a costume change if and when it comes to that. We've seen her run in heels, we know she can, but she might not want to crawl in a faux dungeon dressed like that. Well. She doesn't want to crawl in a faux dungeon at all, but the game is the game.

"How'd it go?" Dolly asks, hopping off the car.

"They were both so sweet," Bristol says, with a particularly sharp smile. "And the entry test was a simple little logic puzzle that I just breezed through, thanks to your tutelage, Bits." She hands me a manila envelope. "One of them gave me his number in case we 'ran into any problems,' which I think perhaps he was not supposed to do. He said his name is *Ant*."

"No, I don't think so." He also wouldn't have given me or Dolly his number, so sending Bristol was the right call either way. I get in the back of the car and open the envelope, sliding out its contents. The welcome letter isn't anything to be concerned with at a glance, but I'll look at it under different lights later, just to be sure. We've got a team AR badge which is also a little GPS/RFID tag so that the gamerunners can keep track of the players, both for safety and planning. I'll look at it more closely later, but from the looks of it, it's factory, hasn't been popped open or anything. There's a cheap cell phone, for similar reasons, I assume. The gamerunners can always call or text a team, and the only number saved in the phone is labeled The Game. There's also, very generous of them I think, a rudimentary flatpack of lock picks, a utility knife, and a game-branded plastic case of band aids.

And, finally, a smaller manilla envelope that points us at the first location. "I thought you were joking about the mineshaft thing," Dolly says, reading over my shoulder.

"I sent you the article about that one game." Years and years ago, and with every game anybody has run thereafter being even more careful and safety-aware, but still. It really sticks out in the narrative.

"Yeah I didn't read it."

"That figures." I though about 50/50 that she would. "Anyway this one is a cave so that they can pretend it's a dungeon crawl. Or that this portion is a dungeon crawl. So not a mine, technically. I guess." Dolly nods, but from her face, she doesn't really know what I mean by this usage of dungeon crawl.

"Shall we, darlings?" Bristol asks, settling herself in the front passenger seat. "Much as I love bickering in parking lots."

"It's almost its own sport," Dolly says, sliding into the driver's seat and starting the car. "Definitely a pastime."

"We're practically specialists by this point," I add, pulling up my VR headset. I want to scout the location and get a sense of the history of it, and I want to see if anybody else playing has posted on social media yet. They probably *shouldn't*, it's better for security, both to keep other players honest and also to prevent outside interference. But it doesn't mean that they *don't*, and during last year's game, or one of last year's games, I tracked the players pretty easily using that. It wasn't this duo's game.

The gussied up cave that we're going to is one that the gamerunners, or the Incorporated Entity of this Game™, bought years ago, and went through extensively, shoring things up and leveling things out and ensuring there were no horrible drops or too tight squeezes or way for it to unexpectedly flood. There are a couple of pictures online from past players, and I circle around local municipal websites until I find the one that it falls under the jurisdiction of, and then root around for the blueprints and permits that would be on file for the kind of work that the game's site describes in the most circumspect of ways. Is having that kind of information on a location cheating? I don't think so, and I don't think the rules speak against it anyway. Maybe it just takes some of the fun out of it.

It's listed as a theme attraction now, like it's part of a park with rides, which is kind of funny. It's got lots of ventilation, it's been checked over for hazardous materials, and is in general as safe as a short network of tunnels in the ground can be made to be. They aren't well lit, of course, but it'd be silly to expect that. Everybody who has a phone has a flashlight, anyway. Has for decades.

"So what do we think the first puzzle'll be?" Dolly asks while I'm doing this.

"Probably we'll have to find and open a locked chest," I say. That's one thing that past players did stick with: none of them posted any of the puzzles they found and solved online, or at least not in unsecured channels.

"Makes sense." I think all of us can lockpick pretty well by this point. Bristol is a quick study in nearly everything. "And you said we won't know how many teams there are?"

"Well not officially, during the game."

"Meaning..."

"Well they gave us this GPS tag which means every team has a GPS tag."

"Uh-huh?" Dolly glances at me over her shoulder as she backs out of the parking spot.

"Which means I can see if I can follow the signal back and then chase who else they're tracing."

"Does it matter, how many other teams there are?" Bristol asks.

"Not particularly." I have a look at our gametag, just with my eyeballs, and then I scan it. It's for both safety tracking and so that it can give updates about how far ahead anybody is, who's gaining on who, to ratchet the tension and competitive spirit, via an app on the provided phone. And it has the team's name. I thought they'd number or color us, but no, there's a name here. If I wanted to, I'm pretty sure it wouldn't take me long to figure out how to nudge our locations, but I don't want to. Yet, anyway. Instead, I mess around until I essentially find the lines of code that broadcast, and then chase that to the game's mainframe, which seems to be an actual mainframe and not just, I don't know, a laptop. A dedicated smartphone. Another thing to look into later.

They've got good security, it would be embarrassing if they didn't. They aren't unfamiliar with the kinds of device vulnerabilities that people (read: people like me, or people like the game participants, I assume) love to exploit when it comes to things like this, and internet of things devices, and the like. I set a dictionary hack to run in the background, and also work out a bit of code to notice when other devices of this type ping home. Then I become aware of Dolly chanting my name and I push my headset up.

"Bits Bits Bits Bits...oh okay."

"Dolly, one sec. Bristol, did they ask you to name the team?"

She smiles, slow and pleased. "They *did*, darling, and we hadn't discussed it ahead of time."

"That's true we didn't."

"Why, what'd she call us?" Dolly asks in a tone of mock horror.

"The Fashion Police."

Dolly brays a laugh. "Seriously?"

"I thought it was a fine name," Bristol says primly. "If we knew we were going to have to come up with a name..."

"No, no, it's fine." Dolly looks back at me. "Right?"

"Yeah, I don't care. It is funny." There was something else. "You were trying to get my attention?"

"Yeah, do you want food or should I just drive?"

"Just drive, I'm going to try and sleep. If you do a drive thru get me something that'll still be okay when I wake up."

"Roger that," Dolly says, sliding on sunglasses. I catch a glimpse of Bristol wrinkling her nose a little, as I lay down across the seats and pull my headset back down. It beats pretty much everything for blocking the light, even in the desert.

Chapter Two

Dolly wakes me up around noon, waving hot fresh french fries under my nose. "I tried to tell her not to, darling," Bristol says in a tone of amused defeat. "But she muttered something about smelling salts, which are not the same at all."

"Yeah but fries are salty, it's practically the same thing," Dolly says, laughing. I sit up and take the fries.

"I think I'm with Bristol on this one."

"Aw come on, Bitsy, did they or did they not work?"

"Not because of the *salt*." I check my programs; I'm not into the mainframe yet, but I did get a pingback on two other teams' game tags, another trio, and also a group of five. On the map, we're only a few miles away from the first location, at an improbable drive thru that used to be a rollerskate drive-in in the nineteen sixties, a non-chain called The Oasis.

"Everybody's against me," she says dramatically, and Bristol purses her lips and looks at the nearby cars to see if anybody is paying attention to us, I guess.

"Honestly, Dolly..."

"Bristles, you need to have some *fun*, okay? We're playing a *game*. Thing." She looks at me.

"It's a game," I mumble around a mouthful of fries.

Bristol sighs, maybe trying to decide which thing to hone in on. Getting Dolly to not call her 'Bristles' has been a losing endeavor, but it's probably the least bothersome of nicknames she could've picked. "You behave as though I never have fun ever," she finally says.

"I mean, no, but yes."

"Dolly, we all just have different kinds of fun," I say.

"With some overlap," she says.

"Okay, when's the last time you suggested something that you thought Bristol would have fun doing?"

She hands a milkshake back to me, but she does look like she's thinking. Bristol looks *very* amused, but waits. I stab a straw into the milkshake.

"We met at that museum!" Dolly says after a while.

"That was my idea," I say, and Bristol lets a smile slowly spread.

"Oh yeah, fair."

"Take your time," Bristol says and Dolly sticks her tongue out.

"Okay fine, we stole that Christmas tree and then went to Marquis' place to make up for—"

"Yes, what a *good* example," Bristol says, clasping her hands together. "What a lovely time that was."

"Best Christmas ever," Dolly agrees. "Are we ready? Bits, you want a burger or anything?"

"No, not right now. Let's go." There aren't many cars, even in the parking lot, and there's nobody around us for miles and miles even on the highway. And then we leave the highway for the first challenge location.

"So we should all three go in, right? Or just two of us?" Dolly asks, standing with her door hanging open. "Maybe we don't want to leave the vehicle. Or all be underground."

"I'll wait with the car," Bristol says. "Because I most certainly don't want to crawl underground if I don't need to."

"Fair enough." Dolly throws her the keys and throws me an I-told-you-so look.

"Vehicle sabotage is unlikely, even if somebody was around," I say. "In addition to being against the rules, it just isn't the tone of the game."

"You said you didn't know who's playin' yet."

"Yeah, that's true, but we're unlikely to be up against my black hat nemesis who can't wait to win by any means necessary."

"Oh, you got one of those?" Dolly's tone is one of idle curiosity, but her eyes sharpen. I can feel Bristol's studied disinterest but absolute focus. "We gonna learn about the seedy underbelly of the hackersphere on this particular road trip?"

"No, I don't have one of those, I was making it up for emphasis."

Dolly waves her hands. "You can't tell me that you hackers don't have any kinds of rivalries going on. I'm sure somebody'd love a chance to take you down a peg."

I blink at her. "Well yes, probably, but my code is all over the place. They wouldn't have to resort to real life situations."

Bristol laughs. "Goodness, do you mean to say that you don't even know who might want to target you, in such an event? Bits, you are a marvel."

I consider possible replies to that statement. "Thanks."

"Well okay, we're burnin' daylight," Dolly says, and heads for the trailhead. I don't bother reminding her that it was her delay, not anybody else's. "You really think these nerds'll use an actual treasure chest in here?" she asks when I catch up.

"I think I'll be disappointed if they don't." I look at the map. "Unless we're misunderstanding what kind of a dungeon they're talking about, and instead it's more like—"

"You know, we've gone a long time without discussing that kind of thing, and it might just be better that way," Dolly says thoughtfully. We keep walking, and then look at each other after a minute and snicker.

"You're probably right though." I don't want to talk about sex dungeons with Dolly. Or anybody, actually. And if it *was* a sex dungeon, we wouldn't be heading underground in the desert, we'd be playing elevator games in the middle of a city. Las Vegas was right there.

They've got a ye olde mineshaft looking entry, but it has a door instead of just being an open hole into the ground, and when Dolly pulls the handle it's locked. Of course it's locked. "Does our thingie unlock it?" she asks, even as she's swiping the badge. I'm about to say no, probably not, but the light on the door goes from red to green and Dolly pulls the door open. "Lookit, I'm a puzzlemaster too."

"See, I knew we'd all pull our weight," I say, and she gestures me ahead of her.

From the door, I almost expected a linoleum floored, fluorescent-lit hallway, but it is a dark tunnel. Dolly's got her flashlight out and on before I do. "Keep your hands free long as you can," she says.

"Okay?" I say, because it does make sense but also I want to know Dolly's reasoning.

"It's a dungeon, right? These nerds—" and then I hear an almost subaudible click as she grabs my shoulder. What looks like a spiky metal ball on a chain releases from the ceiling up by the wall and swings across the tunnel, and when it finishes its arc on the other side, one comes down from there too, and they both swing for a while before stopping. "See?"

"I think they're probably foam," I say. "But yeah, you're right. Obviously." I crouch down and find the place on the floor that triggered the trap, and then fiddle with the settings in my contacts until I find a spectrum of light that can see whatever otherwise invisibly lights up their sensors.

"Maybe they bought the setpieces from American Gladiators or something." The spiky balls have come to a swaying halt in the middle of the tunnel, and Dolly prods at one.

"That show's probably due for a revival again soon, right?" I ask as we move past. I look at the floors but also the walls; they probably won't have the same kind of trigger twice in a row.

"Yeah, hopefully. It's currently an untapped market."

"It might be unfair for you to audition for a thing like that."

"It would *absolutely* be unfair for me to audition for a thing like that," she laughs. "Completely. It'd be a Bristol level fireworks show."

"It's fun to swap roles sometimes," I mutter, stopping to look at a glowing spot on the ceiling up ahead. "Can you see that?"

"I don't think we're ever gonna have *you*...wait you mean...no see what?"

"Okay just wondered." I look at the ground under the spot on the ceiling.

"Would it be in poor taste if they drop us in a hole after what you told me about that historic game?" Dolly drawls. She sounds like she's turned around and looked back behind us.

"Yeah." I dig in my pockets for a laser pointer, pull out a red one first, consider, keep looking until I find my green one instead. I go a couple of steps closer for the better angle, and then flick my laser beam across the point in the ceiling. It stops glowing, and the whole place gets quieter; I hadn't realized that there'd been an ambient sound, maybe of running water, until it was gone. I think all of us have a certain level of static in our hearing at all times. Well, maybe not Bristol. Dolly probably definitely has tinnitus, I can't remember if we've ever talked about it. Or maybe she's never not had tinnitus and didn't realize. "Okay."

"What the fuck was that?"

"A water hazard? Maybe?" The noise doesn't restart, and we walk to the spot, and then through it, with no ill effects. I wonder if we're going to have to walk back through here, or if the tunnels will loop and drop us back at the entrance.

She laughs. "Hey wouldn't it be funny if one of the puzzles was just mini golf?"

"Be careful what you wish for. That'll be the kind of thing that Bristol just beats our pants off at."

"I dunno, I still think that'd be fun *and* funny. Don't you like mini golf?" We come to a fork in the tunnels, and she shines her flashlight one way, and then the other. "Flip a coin?"

"Sure, let me get out my lucky quarter," I say.

"The ecig machine gave me change in gold dollars for some reason. I guess it's kind of fitting here?" She gets one out, balances it on her thumb. I don't ask what ecig machine, it was probably when I was asleep. She had normal cigarettes this morning.

"Uh, heads left, tails right," I say, and she flips, catches it, slaps it on the back of her hand.

"That's heads but who *is* that?" Dolly hands it to me.

"Ida B. Wells?" She shrugs. "Civil rights activist and journalist."

"Oh cool." The left tunnel leads us down further, the air getting cooler and damper. "Hey do you think—" and then there's a click and the floor crumbles away and turns into a slide, shooting us down another hundred feet or so, the walls smooth, nothing to grab onto to slow our momentum. Then there's a short drop, just limbs flailing in the air, and we hit the ground, Dolly's elbow in my ribs, my knee in her back. Then her flashlight clunks down next to us, beam shining on a wooden treasure chest, a web of infrared beams around it.

"Are you okay?" I ask, rolling off of her and getting up. I feel okay, just startled. One of my elbows stings, and I brush some gravel out of it. She pops up too, grabs the flashlight. "I'm okay."

"Yeah, shit, that'll wake you up." She takes a step towards the box and stops. "Okay now what."

"Now I figure out how to disable the security on the box and we open the box."

"What's it gonna do? Shoot us with foam darts? Open spider vents on us? Fill the room with water and then drain us back out at the entrance?"

"We're lower than the entrance."

"I'm sure science could find a way."

"I know your point is that those are mostly funny, non-lethal things, but I do want to figure out the security."

I hear her shrug. "Suit yourself. Do you care if I smoke?"

"Ecig should be fine, sure." I don't know what it could hurt, it's water vapor in an already damp environment, and the vapor is unlikely to interact with the box anyway. The box itself doesn't look locked, so the idea is that somebody will reach unsuspecting through the security grid and then...what? I walk around it at a respectful distance, and finally in the back corner, almost against the wall, I can see where the dirt is disturbed just a little bit. I crouch down and blow on it a little, clearing a view of the power supply. I blow on it again, and there's the infrared transmitter. Or, one of the transmitters. I sit back on my heels and squint; at this angle, there's kind of a too-smooth square of dirt around the chest, that you also aren't supposed to notice, in your focus on the goal. Low-level electrical shock? Maybe? It would really be dampened by the soles of most shoes, though.

This trap isn't online in any way, which is interesting. Though I guess they wanted to make sure nobody caught it by seeing stray code in the air. The gamerunners would know to come reset it based on entry and exit of players. Wire cutters would be super simple. Or, no, I'll splice into the microcontroller, it won't take me long to just alter the pattern long enough to access the chest, then put it back how we found it, leaving the room still set, to all appearances. That would be nicer than making them rewire it, anyway.

I unroll my likeliest set of tools and get on my belly near the base of the thing. Dolly smokes her ecigarette and shifts her weight once in a while, but she's strangely good at waiting. I guess that comes from the sniper training. Or programming.

I've got a juiced up smartphone that's a good enough microcomputer, and after a while I've got things connected and figured out and peel the grid down off the box. "Okay."

"Bits, everything you just did is invisible. It's like the most complicated mime act."

"Oh yeah, sorry. There's an infrared grid that I think will light the floor up with a certain amount of voltage. But that's rerouted for right this second."

She exhales, putting her ecigarette away. "Yeah what's a little light electrocution amongst friends."

"You and Nicolai had a taser duel."

"Exactly." She comes over and opens the box, peers inside. I wonder what's going on with her flashlight, if both her hands are full, but it's hooked onto the front of her utility vest somehow. "It's a lunchbox?"

"There's a joke involved, I'm sure. Just grab it, and we'll figure out the next location back at the car."

"Copy that." She doesn't pick it up by the handle, though, she reaches in with both hands and pulls it out, keeping it level. She glances down at me. "Just in case."

"I wasn't going to say anything. Is there anything else in the box?"

"Not that I can see." Hmm, good point. I stand up and have a peek myself but no, nothing. No message on the inside of the lid, no hidden compartment inside.

"Okay, we're good I guess." I kneel down again and reset the grid, then carefully remove my connectors. You can see the slightly brighter marks, if you look closely, but all in all, not damagingly intrusive. I even scuff the dirt back into the right place. "Now what?"

"Judging from where the vapor went, the exit's over there," Dolly says with a jerk of her chin. I lead the way and we come to what seems like a rock face, but when I run my fingers along it,

I can feel the thrum of electricity. Some patience and vectoring, and I find the catch that triggers the door to slide open, and we walk up what had been the righthand passage, and then walk out of the place, remembering to trick the laser on that one trap a second time.

Outside, Bristol's in the car with all of the windows open, flicking through one of her glossy magazines while talking on the phone. When she looks up and sees us coming, she says "Here they are, Marquis darling, I'm going to let you go. Yes, I did enjoy catching up. Yes, I *do* hope to see you next month in Venice."

"Glad you weren't too worried," Dolly says. She starts to put the lunchbox on the hood of the car then stops, looks around, and picks a nearby boulder instead.

"It probably isn't a bomb," I say.

"Can't be too careful."

"Is that a princess lunchbox?" Bristol asks, getting out of the car. "What happened? You're both absolutely covered in dirt! Like you were—"

"In a cave?" Dolly asks, smirking, and Bristol laughs.

"Just so."

"Super scandalous for the fashion police, right? Like, they'll come and take our badges away if—"

"No, the oversight for the fashion police doesn't issue physical badges," Bristol says smoothly, winking at me. "They can disable them remotely."

"Well I guess you told me, princess."

Chapter Three

I t *is* a princess lunchbox, not any specific character who falls under copyright, probably from a five dollar store or something. Inside is a half gallon sized, resealable silicon bag like you'd have for kitchen stuff, and inside of *that* is a notecard with the clue to the next location. I guess that water hazard can get out of control.

I check on my running code; two more teams, both also trios. The progress bar on the mainframe is almost full, but that can be misleading, that just means it thinks that it's getting close to what the password is, based on how many characters it thinks the password is (seventeen) and how much time has elapsed (five hours.) There can be one or more further layers of security that set me back, there could be two-factor authentication to try and figure out, the list goes on. I do know that people tend not to use biometric security, because it still isn't protected by the Fourth Amendment and is unlikely to be in our lifetime.

"Well okay, so what does this mean?" Dolly asks, handing the card to me. "Riddles aren't my thing."

"Far from the Magic Kingdom and too late for Burning Man, there's still enchantment to be found in the desert," I read out loud. "I don't know. There's a lot of desert. Maybe—"

"Honestly, girls, they mean the Seven Magic Mountains art installation." Dolly looks at her blankly, so she's got that part covered, and I look it up online instead and plot the route. Back the way we came, of course, and then further south still.

"See, Bristles, you've got *culture*, I've always said that we appreciate that about you."

"Have you?" Bristol smiles one of her particular smiles, but she is clearly pleased. If it wasn't weird I'd number and label them sometime, because a certain array of her smiles are practiced and calculated.

"Well not when you can hear me, that's not how that kind of compliment works."

"Of course not," Bristol says, still smiling. "Shall we, then? And we need to stop at a package pickup, I ordered more sunscreen. Somehow, I'd wildly underestimated how much I thought we would need."

"We?" I ask.

"If we're going to be driving around together solving riddles for an indeterminate amount of time while slathered in sufficient amounts of sunscreen, yes no matter how tan you are already hush Dolly, you will not do so while smelling like drugstore no-name brands. So yes. We." Dolly snaps her mouth shut. That might've been the first time Bristol has ever commented on either of our skin tones. Bristol looks at her, and then at me. "Does that seem fair?"

"I don't mind, I was just surprised." I could know how much Bristol's sunscreen costs in thirty seconds, but it's fun to imagine how much instead. Thirty dollars a tube? Or whatever the containment is. Fifty?

"Well let's hit the road then. This is a race too, isn't it? Plus we have to feed Bits."

"I had fries?"

"Yeah but usin' all that brain power needs more calories."

"Dolly, if you're hungry again you can just say so," Bristol says. "And we'll buy more water too."

"Sure thing, queen of the desert." For all their bickering, I think I've only seen Dolly actually mad at Bristol one time, and right now, we aren't even close. This is just recreational, and apparently how they communicate best.

WE GO THROUGH THE OASIS again, and again miss out on the rollerskating waitstaff experience, but their fries are really good, so I'm happy for the repeat. Bristol less so, but she's had lots of opportunity to add snacks that she deems acceptable to her sunscreen order. It's while we're driving to that package pickup location that she suddenly says, with suspicion, "How will we be arranging accommodations for the night, with all this bouncing about? We don't even know where we'll go after the installation."

"Well that's the thing about these kinds of events," I say carefully. "They're not officially serial all-nighters, that can't really be safely condoned, but most of the time nobody like, gets rooms or anything."

Dolly keeps quiet, checking me in the mirror occasionally, containing her smirk, while Bristol mulls this over. "And how long did last year's event run?"

I already know, but take a little bit of time, like I'm looking it up. "The winning team finished in 53 hours and change, and the final team finished in 78 hours."

"I see."

"Teams still bother to finish, after the first three?" Dolly asks.

"Well yeah. Wouldn't you?" I don't really understand the question. Yes, winning and doing well are important, but sometimes when you start a thing, you just have to finish the thing.

"Yeah, I guess I would. Sometimes you just gotta see something through to the bitter end." We laugh, even though it isn't really quite a joke, I don't think. She looks over at Bristol. "Just gotta add dry shampoo to your order, I guess." Bristol gives the slightest of shudders.

THE PACKAGE PICKUP location is an unstaffed, multi-purpose rest stop, a bank of car chargers facing a bank of vending machines and restrooms, asphalt in between, locked delivery boxes at the far end.

"Want to make bets on how long she'll last without stopping for a hotel or anything?" Dolly asks when I walk out of the bathroom. She's studying the canned coffee machine, already holding a snack bag.

"No. Bristol always finds a way to rise to an occasion."

"Maybe you're right." She considers, nodding, then pushes a couple of buttons on the machine and a coffee kachunks out for her. "We've still got laws about labeling right?" She shows me the can; Nitro Himalayan™ butter* coffee.

"Much as they've ever worked, yeah. What's it say when you chase the asterisk?" It's also weird enough to be tempting and I might as well try it, and she squints at the tiny writing on the can while I get my own.

"It's a plant-based butter, not authentically from yaks. Oh, *and* it's made with genetic engineering. That's a separate line, not the butter specifically."

"Ooh I love genetic engineering." I eye the QR code on the can until it scans and pops up all that info for me in AR, crisp and zoomable. Something about these cans almost always ends up weirdly overprinted, like they got sprayed twice just slightly offset, or somebody knocked the machine at just the wrong time. Maybe a hurricane passed over and the automated factory kept running because the wind didn't trip the sensors. Or the employees weren't allowed to leave.

"Right? It's our favorite." She pops the tab, waits a second while the nitro thing makes its noise, and then takes a swig, kind of tilts her head this way and that like Bristol at a wine tasting, and I laugh. "Well it's obviously not the real thing. Like really really obviously. But the nitro thing helps with the texture, I think?"

I pop the tab on my own and smell it. Smells like nitro and vegetable yak butter. "Have you had the real thing?"

"Yeah, haven't you?" She watches my face as I try it. The nitro and not-butter do combine to make that supposed-to-be-velvety texture but it also isn't quite correct.

"I've had what a cafe called bulletproof coffee, which amounted to the same thing. Plus I think it's normally tea that they use in—"

"Well yeah of course it is. But I've had the tea, is what I mean."

"In the Himalayas?" I only have the loosest of reckonings of Dolly's global travel. Bristol's, more so, because she'll talk about it in some detail with frequency. Dolly, you just get the occasional sporadic anecdote of taser duels and sturgeon fishing and cliff diving and now drinking Himalayan butter tea in the Himalayas.

"Yeah, one of my buddies was going to summit Everest and I went to see him off."

I take a moment to process that because again, one of Dolly's buddies could be any category of people from various job fields and locales. "Did he?"

"Did he what? Did he make it? Wow what a question. Yeah, he made it up. Back down off the mountain too, hardly anybody ever talks about that. That you gotta walk back down, after you summit Everest."

"You're right, they don't." I mean, they must. But I'm not into mountaineering, I've never seen even the most idle comment of coming back down off the mountain.

"Anyway he stuck around there and hooked up with one of those groups that does garbage runs, because people just fucking dump trash all over that mountain an' it's disgusting. There oughta be a law."

"Dolly, calling for laws? You feeling okay?" I drink more of my coffee and check out the snacks. One of the machines is ocean themed, weird choice for the middle of the desert or maybe not; dried shrimp, and squid, and seaweed snacks. Another one is cricket chips and corn chips, and cricket corn chips, and that's what Dolly's bag is from. Finally, there is a candy one, chocolate and fake chocolate and a surprising range of gummies. She keeps chattering about environmentalism of all things, and I get a bag of what claims to be up to* 100 gummy flavors but probably doesn't contain 100 total gummies so we'll see how that goes.

"What alarming things are you two getting?" Bristol asks.

"Do you like Himalayan butter beverages?" Dolly asks, holding out her can. Bristol looks at it, pursing her lips a little as she reads the label.

"Not in my experience, but thank you," she says.

"We're over here swishing our canned coffee for the bouquet and Bristol's all 'bestie, not even once,'" Dolly says to me in a confidential tone.

"I don't think they canned coffee with beans that Bristol would prefer," I say.

"Definitely not nitro canned coffee," Dolly says.

"Oh definitely not."

"Are you two quite through?" Bristol asks, but she's smiling. The curiosity has gotten the better of her, or it's something she's had before, and she's gotten a chocolate croissant from one machine and a bottle of milk tea from another. I saw her look at the sushi machine, but it very diligently has a date and time for when the contents were placed in the machine and the buttons are all dark; it wouldn't let you buy even if you wanted to.

Dolly chugs the rest of her coffee and tosses it into the recycle bin. "Yeah, let's get back on the road. We were waiting for you."

Bristol rolls her eyes. "Of course you were."

Chapter Four

While we're en route to the art installation, I do the VR experience to try and assess where I think the clue might be. It seems likely that it's in the retro museum tour headsets that are there for guests; it would be the least invasive thing that they could do. Interfering with the exhibit would be against the game's own rules, and probably laws too, if they were worried about that. I know that they're concerned with their rules, anyway.

According to the website, the installation hasn't always had headsets that visitors could use, in museum tour fashion, because it previously relied on smartphone apps. But thanks to a donor a few years back, they had them available now. According to the website, the installation has been maintained for many years beyond its original inception, and there's talk of leaving a virtual experience if it's ever physically dismantled. Bristol hasn't said if she's visited it before, but I don't think that's a necessary detail. The tour headsets will all look the same, or they won't. There will be an indeterminate number available, and we'll have to quickly get through them to get to the right one.

My phone vibrates; another team identified.

"Hey wouldn't it be funny if we were playin' against one of your nemeses or something," Dolly asks, as we pull into the parking area.

I blink at her. "One of my nemeses?"

"Yeah, isn't that a thing you nerds do? Have nemeses? Rivals? Competition?"

"Other than the competition we're in right now."

"Yeah." She parks, and exchanges a look with Bristol. "Nobody's coming to mind?"

"No. Are you hinting at something?" I look out the rearview window, in case somebody's standing there with a gun, wearing a t-shirt that says 'I'll get you, Bits!' but nobody's there. Nobody else is in the parking area, actually. I look back at them. "What?"

"I just find it hard to believe that you don't have anybody who thinks you're their nemesis or rival or whatever. If I search it online, do you think it'll come up?"

I laugh. "Dolly, you're ridiculous."

"She does have an interesting point, darling," Bristol says, and I wonder if that's it. Dolly's trying to keep Bristol engaged.

"Yeah, search it online, see if anything comes up. Me and Bristol will check out the tour recordings for the clue." Oh, I didn't tell them that part. "Because there aren't any guides or signs, they have recorded material for visitors, and I think that's where the clue will be."

"Yes, let's," Bristol says. Dolly shrugs and runs her window down, digging out her phone with one hand and her ecigarette with the other.

"I'll let you know what I find," she says.

"Thanks a bunch, Dolly," I say, and Bristol laughs. We get out of the car, and she stops me, pulling out one of her containers of sunscreen.

"Hold out your arms," she says, and gives me a spray, top to bottom. "Rub it in on your face."

"Thanks." It smells lightly floral, I don't know what kind.

"You're welcome. Though honestly, Bits, I don't know how you can be so confident," she says as we walk towards the rack where the recordings are.

"Having a rival or nemesis or whatever wouldn't mean that it puts me in personal danger. It's not like if people just started showing up to taser duel Dolly or something."

"I think if people with a vendetta against Dolly were to appear, it wouln't be tasers that they wielded," Bristol says.

"You're probably right." I survey the tour headsets; they're made to look like tape decks, but nobody's made cassettes in a really long time. They've come back and gone out again two or three times since the early aughts. The headphones material is antibacterial, and there's a wipes and hand sanitizer station nearby. "Seven statues," I say.

"There aren't really statues, they're painted stacks of rock," Bristol says.

"True." But she's still talking and I'm counting the row of headset tours, and there are eight here, one and two doubled up on the same hook. I pick up the seventh in line, and then I pick up the eighth one, to spot the differences. Seven is heavier, actually, it's a metal tape deck spray-painted white to match the plastic of the others, and I slide the headphones on. I hear Bristol break off speaking abruptly, but I'm also pulling up my

VR headset so that I can record whatever the tape says, in case it self destructs or we want to refer back to it or whatever.

Whoever recorded it clearly listened to the actual tour; it even starts the same way, but the voice is all wrong. Then they have a static effects noise, like a radio getting garbled between stations, and then the voice says "Good job, player, you've found the clue. The next location doesn't allow earthly visitors, but things are different if you're out of this world." The static plays again, with whistling noise layered into it, and then it's some more of the tour before cutting off to dead air.

"Was that it? Have we gotten the clue?" Bristol asks, when I pull the headphones off.

"Yeah, but I don't think you're going to know this one," I say. I pull one of the wipes out of the dispenser and swipe it over the headphones, then pull another and wipe down the body of the tape deck as I hang it up.

Bristol quirks her lips. "Well why not?"

"Let's go back to the car and I'll play it for both of you." I almost want to look around, to see if there's another component here, but I don't think there is. I think they think what they said was enough, and I'm drawing an immediate blank, but that whistling is familiar. And the person I associate with whistling most is in the car not far from here.

Dolly's still in the same place, which isn't to say she didn't get out and spy on us from afar while we were at the exhibit, but if she did that, she made it back to the car without any of us seeing. We get in the car, Bristol in the front and me in back. I seem to remember her saying something about never getting to ride in front, and I hadn't realized it bothered her. And especially on trips like this, I like being able to stretch out on the seat anyway.

"Okay, so what's the story?" Dolly asks. "Was that it?"

I pull up my headset and make it talk to the car's bluetooth. "Listen." I play the clue, then rewind it just to the whistle and play that again.

"Bits, I apologize, you are entirely correct. I don't know this one."

We look at Dolly, who looks thoughtful. "Play it again." I do. "It prob'ly won't change anything, but can you get rid of the static?"

"I think so?" I mess around with the recording for a little while and get the layers peeled apart, and play just the whistling.

Dolly nods. "The answer's gotta be Area 51, right?"

"Does it?" Bristol asks, eyebrows raised. I wonder if she knows what Area 51 is; it's hard to parse what I think is and isn't common knowledge, after a certain point.

"There's a real old show the guys used to watch, that's still too new for you to like it, Bristles, so no wonder you don't know it. But it was about government conspiracies, so it was a nice in-joke for us to watch episodes in our downtime. And that's part of the theme song. So, that plus the words and bam, Area 51." She starts the car.

Bristol's still sideways in her seat, and she looks back at me. "Do you agree?"

"I can verify now, anyway." I look up the show, listen to the theme song. "Yeah, okay." I run it through the car speakers.

"Excellent work, Dolly," Bristol says appreciatively, as she settles into her seat and fastens the seatbelt.

—————— ┼┼\╵┼┤ ——————

DRIVING BACK AND FORTH across Nevada gives some stark landscape, but also some pretty stuff. Almost alien in and of itself; it'd be easy to film a Mars movie out here or something. Or maybe a Mars landing conspiracy theory movie, wouldn't that be fun? I take some recordings, because every once in a while it's fun to tinker with video game engines and builders, even if I'm not all that creative. Plus, Creative Commons and stock photo sites could always use more available material.

Bristol hums to herself a little, occasionally, as she responds to messages and I think scrolls articles online. I'm not watching her, per se, I just know that's her typical habit. Who knew that 'being a socialite' was still a real thing, in this day and age? But that's what Bristol is, in addition to the whole heist and thievery thing. And running The Game, though I'm pretty sure she would never have done this if we didn't ask. It's social currency; she has a little bit of leverage now, if there's a job or whatever that she wants to do but we don't. I can understand that, it's fine.

"So what're we gonna do when we get to Area 51 and it's, y'know, a military installation that doesn't allow visitors?" Dolly asks.

"Well I don't imagine the gamerunners went to Area 51, Dolly, they probably went to the nearest bar," Bristol says without looking up.

Dolly glances at me in the rear view. "On it," I say. There's three to five near-ish bars or bar restaurants, depending on how you're counting, and only one of them has a menu online, so I put that in the GPS for Dolly. "Yes they have burgers."

"Oooh," Dolly says at the same time Bristol sort of sniffs.

"They do call the appetizers 'starters' if that helps at all, Bristol," I say.

"Helps *what*?" Dolly asks.

"That they don't call them something appalling like snackatizers," Bristol says.

"What's it matter? It's the same stuff. It means the same thing."

"It's an *awful* word."

Dolly looks at her for a little too long, frowning, before looking at the road again. "How can a word be terrible? It's just a word. It's not a slur or anything, it's a whatchamacallit, a portmanteau of snacks and appetizers. Snackatizers."

"It sounds vulgar."

"It does *not*, Bristles, come off it." Dolly's laughing now, though.

"Not vulgar like, shouldn't be said in polite company just. Crass. No, perhaps that isn't what I mean either."

"You mean low class," I say helpfully. "You mean it sounds cheap."

Dolly looks at Bristol's face and laughs again. "She's got you there."

"Perhaps I thought it was impolite to be so snobby," Bristol says primly.

"Sure, but ain't it what you mean?"

A pause, a test; if Bristol calls Dolly on 'ain't' she's even snobbier. "Yes, I suppose it is what I mean," Bristol says finally. "I do hope you're satisfied."

"*Quite* satisfied," Dolly says. "Can we order ahead, or should we wait until we're there?" she asks me. "To spare Bristol's sensibilities." It's very quiet, but I think I hear Bristol laugh.

"Probably wait," I say. "We'll want to find the clue first, and they're open late anyway."

"What a relief," Bristol says.

"Do we wanna guess what we'll have to look for? Skywriting? A simulated UFO crash? Blacklight on the rocks?"

"I think it'll have to be small," I say. "Or subtle, anyway. So no fiery crash reenactments probably."

"Ah well, a girl can dream, right Bristles?"

"Of course, Dolly darling."

WE DRIVE UP THE ASSUMED stretch of road and then back down again, and then Bristol points at a newspaper vending machine rack that's in a puddle of light at a convenience store. I guess it's been the whole day, I shouldn't say it's dark 'already' but it feels like already. "That isn't real," she says.

"Looks pretty real," Dolly says, but she's already pulling over.

"The paper that uses that coloring and masthead isn't called that, though," Bristol says. I take a screenshot and search, but she's right, and I get out to go investigate.

"Hold up," Dolly says, and hops out too, leaving the car on.

"It's out in the open, they can't booby trap it."

"Still." We both give it a quick visual once-over, and then she pulls on the handle and it's locked. "They seriously want you to pay for the fake newspaper?"

"Well I'm sure they *want* us to," I say, looking at the coin slot. I don't always carry around slugs of all sizes, but this seemed like a good time to have all my niche stuff on hand. I can also then just pop the lock and get my slugs back, and I feed them into the machine one by one, until the latch clicks. "Here." I hand it to Dolly and get out my lockpicks.

"How many newspapers do you think Bristol is like, familiar with at a glance. Is that weird?"

"We've all got our skills," I say, setting the pins and opening the lock without difficulty; if nothing else, I thought it might have rusted or something. It seems like an older model, a lot of them will take a chip now. "See anything apparent in the paper?"

"Not at a glance, but I'm not a newshound, so who knows."

"Even if you were, I think we're all up on different kinds of news." My slugs are the only thing in the cash box, and I take them and close the thing up again before opening the game app on the provided phone and texting the saved number that we got the clue. I wonder why they didn't create an app, it would've been simple enough. It might've also further fueled the competition, to see the progress bars of the other teams. Maybe they wanted to keep it just analog enough, who can say.

I stand up and hold my hand out for the paper, and when Dolly hands it over, something falls out on the ground. Another manilla envelope, and nothing is written on either side, when I pick it up and turn it over. The newspaper's real masthead, fake title matches the one on the vending machine, and isn't that interesting, that they printed a whole very short fake newspaper but didn't program an app. The title story is about declassified government documents about UFOs, as if that was big news and not something they've been doing periodically since the twenties.

We go back to the car and turn on the dome light. I open the envelope, which contains two pieces of paper that have pictures of regular-seeming individual keys on them. Dolly hands Bristol the newspaper to peruse and takes out her ecigarette. "What's that?" she asks.

"Somebody's house keys? I'm not sure yet."

Bristol pages through the paper. "These are all articles from online," she says. "Mostly about alien conspiracies. But there is an advertisements section in the back, perhaps that's where our clue is? Otherwise I'm at a loss." She hands the paper to me.

It feels like a newspaper should, they had it printed someplace pulpily authentic, but each article has its separate sourced website at the bottom of it. The ads also seem like very normal newspaper sorts of ads, used cars and a refrigerator and some personals. At first I concentrate on the personals, that seems like the stereotypical place where they put clues in old spy movies, isn't it? But there's almost no information there, clue-y or otherwise; I wonder if those are real or if the gamerunners made them up, and which would be worse.

"Okay I've got no idea," I say. "Other than that the clue is here." My phone pings; I've got all of the team information now. I close the alert, I'll look at that after we finish this. Then I'll be able to tell Dolly if I've got somebody who thinks they're my nemesis or not on an opposing team.

"How 'bout we get food before that place closes and maybe it'll come to us."

"A proper sit down meal. I'm not eating in the car with food balanced on my knees," Bristol says.

"You did this morning."

"My limit for that activity is once per day."

"Of course, princess, sorry." But Dolly's grinning, not put out by this really, and Bristol laughs.

Chapter Five

Dolly and I get burgers and fries and Bristol gets fish and chips. Our fries do all look the same, for the record. We also get a basket of fried pickle chips that she looks askance at, but does take a few. Dolly and I meet eyes briefly, but we don't say anything; we've never seen Bristol have so much fried food on her plate at once, and don't want to break the spell.

I entertain a brief mental fantasy that Bristol isn't Bristol, and has actually been replaced with an AI copy that they first engineered back when she was in detention at that black site, and then perfected the body over time, and finally thought it was time to deploy after she pepper sprayed Will after that wedding. Poor Will.

But it's an interesting thought; how would we know Bristol was really Bristol? Or any of us, for that matter. We've spent a lot of time together, but enough time to know the difference from computer generated copies? I guess depending on the copy. Depending on the person.

"Should we have come up with a pass phrase before now?" I ask, and judging from their faces, eyebrows raised almost the same exact way, that's nowhere in the ballpark of where the conversation had been.

"Maybe, Bitsy, but why complicate things?"

"I guess you're right," I say.

"Though we could do that, darling, if it'll make you feel better," Bristol says, folding her napkin and setting it on the table again. It's a paper napkin but she still does it.

"I guess we'll think about it. Maybe implement it after this." I appreciate that they just know we're on different trains of thought sometimes, it can be hard to reconcile.

"How do we think the other teams're doing?" Dolly asks after a few minutes have passed, and the waitress clears our things away.

"Oh that's right, I've got the lists now. And I could scope out how many clues they've each gotten."

"If we have any sort of a margin, might we be permitted a hotel room for a few hours?" Bristol asks in a very slightly wheedling tone.

Dolly shrugs. "I guess. If we're good enough."

I don't put on my VR headset in the restaurant, I just get out my phone and swipe through the data. I do see names that I recognize just from the hackersphere in general, but nobody I really know to talk to. No names that I have flagged, red or otherwise. "Looks like everybody else has done their second clue, and we're the only ones who've logged reaching their third."

"Seeing any overlap yet?"

"One other team has done our first clue now, as their second."

"Hmm," Dolly says, and Bristol glances at her pleadingly. "Okay fine we'll stop for the night, but we're up early."

"Of course, darling," she says.

BRISTOL VETOES THE first motel option without even saying a word; Dolly pulls into the parking lot, looks at her face, laughs, and gets back on the road. The hotel we reach next isn't as bad, or is good enough, which are about the same thing I guess. We just get one room, with a cot, and while Bristol does her evening preening, I just sack out on the cot.

I check my messages to see if there's anything I need to pay attention to right away but it's mostly a lot of junk, no action items. I'm still not in the gamerunners' mainframe but that's okay, it'll be soon I think.

I look at the list of other teams now, ten total. Some of them have named themselves very obvious online gamer clan tag sorts of things, and one of them might be a band, they're named after a band. None of it seems particularly notable, and they're all miles and hours away from us, and I scroll through the team rosters, mostly handle-style names and not like, first-and-last, which makes sense, given the territory and nature of the competition. None of them look familiar, but that isn't really a surprise; even if you narrow all of the billions of people in the world down to just the hackers, there's still a lot. But it's been a long day, both physically and mentally, and I really need to sleep or else I'm really a hypocrite for saying anything to Dolly about it.

I leave the headset on, because I do most nights anyway, and as I'm drifting off, I hear Dolly drop her boots on the floor, and dimly hear Bristol take a call. From Marquis I think, but I'm only catching the occasional word in addition to darling.

The way she says darling to Marquis is different from how she says it to Dolly is different from how she says it to Will. I've got an ever-updating table of the situations where Bristol calls us, and other people, darling; it's got a vocal scale rating of 1-5. This was about a 2. She's kind of stressed, but in the way she gets stressed when in underperforming accommodations after being in the car with Dolly all day. But there's a way she says it when she means it, to people she ostensibly cares about, and there's a way she says it to people that she wants to think she cares about, and the nuance is very slim. It's been an interesting pattern to observe and track. She'll say darling when she wants to smooth things over and want somebody to not be mad at her, or when she wants people to feel as though they're in her confidence and soften towards her. It's only rarely that I've heard somebody snap back at her, don't call me darling. Or, I never have, actually, thinking back. But it has to have happened, I think. It's almost impossible for it to not have happened.

I don't dream anything, or if I do, I don't remember. Dolly's quiet when she gets up, but I wake up anyway when she turns on the shower. Bristol doesn't move until she starts whistling, though. She moves, maybe to check the time, and sighs a little before sitting up. It's 5:30; Dolly did promise early, and I don't know if she's like this because she's just always been like this, or if it's from the secret super soldier training program or a combination of the two. It's probably a combination of the two; she mentions brothers often enough that we'll probably meet them sooner or later, and I'm sure they'll be the same way. Though I think some of them were also in the program, like Butler, so we really will never know.

There's a rustle of paper, and I sit up and pull my headset off. Bristol is flicking through the pages of the clue newspaper again. She looks up at me and asks, "Are these real estate listings genuine, or fake?"

I get up to come look, and there's a grid of houses on one of the pages. None of them have any more page space than the others, and they all seem normal enough. I don't know anything about real estate in the area, but I don't really need to. A couple of quick seconds searching, and these are all real addresses, on realtor websites. I find one of those real estate aggregate sites that lists them all on a map and look at it; one of them, while still in a neighborhood, seems to have more land surrounding it than the others. A long driveway and more tree cover.

"This might be it," I say, tapping on the paper.

"Kinda risky, isn't it?" Dolly asks. I didn't notice her come out of the bathroom, but she's toweling her hair off and watching us.

"Maybe one of them is a real estate agent," I say. "So they've got the keys to all these places."

"We've already established that many of *us* don't need keys," Bristol says.

"No, but when they've already made it so easy, why not go along with it?" One of us threw a coffee can in the wastebasket and I take it out and go to the bathroom to rinse it. "Plus, they might have tried to set up trappy protections against people using picks, as an elimination tactic."

"Do people normally get eliminated from these games?" Dolly asks.

"Once in a while. It's all supposed to be sportsmanlike and in good fun, but also this one has the rewards it does, so..."

"It may have attracted an unsavory element?" Bristol asks. She's getting out her toiletries and who knows how long that'll take. I'm sure her 'drive around to play a clue game' skin care and makeup routine is a little less involved than it would be for going out to an art gallery or a date, but I also can't reliably tell the difference.

"Something like that." I've got tin snips in my toolkit, and they both watch me in silence for a few minutes.

"You done that before, Bitsy?"

"Yeah, have you?"

"Not successfully, just screwin' around because somebody watched a video online." Hair dry enough, apparently, Dolly's scraping it back into a ponytail. Bristol watches her but doesn't say anything. I'm sure Bristol has fashion plates ready to go, mentally, with how she'd do us up given the opportunity. The closest she's come so far was being able to tell us to have suits to be her bodyguards when she was playing rich fiancée, and even then, I'm not sure how necessary the suits were after all. Like, she was sure in danger at least once, but it wasn't anything the suits helped with.

"How else would one solve that particular bit of the clue?" Bristol asks.

"There are places online that you can give a picture of keys and they'll send you one, but it takes at least a couple of days, I think. I've never done it. I guess you could also use a bump key. Without seeing their setup, if we even take the time to look at it, I don't know if a bump key is more risky than picking or less. I don't know if any of it is risky, and that's probably part of the game."

"Probably, yes," Bristol says, and goes to the shower.

BRISTOL DOESN'T WEAR heels today, and Dolly and I somehow don't say anything about the boots she's wearing instead. I'm also not sure if what she's wearing is a dress or a romper or what, but that's not my business. She's also got her hair in a ponytail but then I think she also curled it or something. Bristol's hair in a ponytail looks different from almost everybody else's hair in a ponytail.

To her credit, she only gives me and Dolly the slightest of despairing looks as we get in the car and swing through a drive thru on the way to the location.

"How are the other teams lookin', Bitsy?" Dolly asks when she hands back my iced coffee and cardboard tube of little hash browns.

"No more clue successes have been logged since last night. Also, I don't think any of them is my nemesis."

"Aw, dang."

"Dolly, why are you so keen on Bits having a nemesis?"

Dolly shrugs. "I just figured that with such a niche thing, there had to be rivalries, right?"

"Perhaps. Do *you* have a nemesis?"

"Oh yeah, I did."

"You...did."

I catch a glimpse of Dolly's grin in the rear view as she glances at Bristol. "Well, yeah. It's not like I could let it keep going."

Bristol waits a few minutes, I think, but Dolly doesn't continue, and she sighs. "Dolly, darling, you simply cannot dangle a story like that and not tell it."

46   JENNIFER R. DONOHUE

"Well yeah I can, it might upset your delicate sensibilities." Bristol sighs again and Dolly laughs. "Okay fine, it was one of our kind of neighbors, before any of us kids joined up with the program. I say kind of neighbor because he didn't really *live* there, he was a rich guy from the city who had a vacant property most of the time and then once in a while came out to get drunk and do stupid weekend shit like drunk fourwheeling, hunting outside his property lines, generally makin' himself a nuisance to the locals."

"If you were so young, was he really your nemesis?" I ask.

"Maybe not by the dictionary definition, I dunno. You look it up if it bothers you so much. Anyway, his disrespect for property lines was personal, he absolutely wanted everybody else to respect *his* property lines, whether they were kids or not, or hunting or not, and there was one genuinely scary time when he ran us off that it seemed like maybe he was gonna do more than yell about it. So I went back that night with a roll of fishing line and put it across one of his four wheeler trails."

"Dolly, you didn't," Bristol says, horrified but rapt.

"Sure did. And he broke his fuckin' neck, coming down that trail at high speed. But if you wondered, breaking your neck doesn't automatically kill you, so he was out there yelling for a while before anybody investigated because, you know. Property lines."

"Jesus Christ, Dolly," I say, when she doesn't keep going.

"What? Oh, we didn't let him like, suffocate to death out there. Somebody went out to check on him eventually and he got airlifted out. Sold the property the next year; the new neighbors were nicer."

We're all quiet for a little while. "Well that's good," I finally say, and Dolly nods, loudly rattling the ice in her cup.

"Yeah, real nice folks. Had dogs, fit in good with the neighborhood. Such as it was. More like a vicinity, not a real neighborhood like you prob'ly grew up in, Bristles."

"I wasn't—"

"No, I know, but it helps paint the mental picture, doesn't it?"

"Yes, darling, it does."

We drive through what Dolly probably calls a real neighborhood, and go past the driveway once, taking a long loop back so as not to draw attention, but I don't even see a single curtain twitch. Surprisingly, this neighborhood is also short on those little yard signs that tell you what kind of surveillance cameras they've got on the front porches, which is probably something the gamerunners also noticed and took into consideration when they picked this location.

No other cars are in the driveway, and when I do a scan, I don't see any active device in the vicinity. The thermostat inside is a smart one, but that's it. Nobody's surveillance around, unless it's offline, no rival teams who hid when we pulled up, nothing. There's even birdsong when we get out of the car.

"How the other half lives," Dolly says, as though we haven't had more money than we know what to do with for a couple of years now.

"Dolly, do you ever think about settling down and starting a family? Perhaps with Butler?" Bristol asks, as we get out of the car and go up the front walk. There's a real estate lockbox on the front door handle, and I guess that's one of the alternatives. If you don't know how to make a key, can't take the time to order one, you maybe know how to get around one of those digital locks to get the house keys from inside.

"With *Butler*?" Dolly almost shriek-laughs, and I blink at my coffee can keys, trying to choose which one is for the door-knob and which is for the deadbolt. "Bristol what the fuck?"

"Well he's clearly smitten with you," Bristol says primly. "But whomever."

"Are you just sayin' that because he wasn't all over you? Are you *jealous*?"

"I am not jealous."

It's kind of funny that this kind of bickering is almost the only way that Bristol and Dolly communicate, but also it works, so who am I to judge? I let their conversation fade in my perception as I get out a penlight and peer into the keyways, look at my keys, and make my choices.

When the locks click and the door swings open, Bristol and Dolly cut off behind me, and I think all of us are looking for an alarm panel to be disabled, but there isn't one. No alarm sounds. The house has that cold bleachy smell of a place that's air conditioned and cleaned regularly, but that nobody's living in. There was a while right when I was getting started with all this that I'd spoof reservations at condos and stuff, and this is what they'd smell like. They'd look like homes, or movie sets of homes, waiting for people to be in them.

The entry hall leads straight back to one of those kitchens with the island, marble countertops, and the refrigerator is hidden as one of the wood-paneled cabinets. I think Dolly once called this a lemonade lady kitchen, when she was describing something. The island has a bouquet of flowers in a vase on it, and an accompanying card. I look back at Bristol and Dolly, and Dolly shrugs but Bristol's the one among us most accustomed to getting flowers and she goes to the bouquet and examines it briefly before picking up the card. Actually, I've never gotten flowers. I can't speak for Dolly.

"Won't the flower means something?" Bristol asks. "I don't think they do in a language of flowers way, I think that might be too involved and get us off track. But do you know anything about desert flora?"

"We don't really need to know about desert flora, we have the internet," I say. I snap a picture and search; the top results are about Death Valley superbloom. I show Bristol and Dolly, who shrugs, and then ask, "What does the card say?"

"It's called the most dangerous eight seconds in sports, but don't worry, we'll cushion your fall." Bristol shrugs a little. "I'm certain it's—"

Dolly laughs. "Are you two kiddin' me?"

"What?" I look at the flowers again, like there's something obvious there, that Dolly sees but we don't.

"The most dangerous eight seconds in sports is *bullriding*," she says. "And those're Death Valley flowers, you said? So that's where we're going and that's what we're doing."

"We are *not* bullriding," Bristol says, blinking.

"Well probably not a *real* one." Dolly looks at me, and I shrug. "Well okay come on, we've got ourselves pointed, anyway."

Chapter Six

We stop to charge the car again. This time, it's in an outlet mall parking lot, and Bristol abandons us for air conditioning and the promise of coach bags and a new bottle of perfume. I check on the other teams. Could I be noting their locations, to make our time easier? Probably, sure, especially since only a couple of them have pinged where we've been so far. Do I want to actually play the game fair and square? Also yes. That probably won't be the case for everybody, but also none of my levels of digital security have been breached yet. I'm not counting the gamerunner tag in this consideration; it's certainly vulnerable, I clocked that immediately. But it won't allow a leapfrog into any of our devices.

That doesn't mean I shouldn't do a scan, now that I'm thinking about it. I've always got security running, of course, and nobody's breached my firewall yet but that doesn't mean it'll never happen. And there's no reason to think that I'm the only one, out of all these teams, doing any kind of hacking up the chain.

At least we don't have to worry about the car. This is one that Dolly and I have worked on, and the engine and security systems are separate from anything that's online. It's still got the GPS sure, but to the outside observer, it looks like a phone GPS or a dedicated unit, it doesn't tell you anything about the car. Some makes and models have a remote killswitch that the cops can subpoena on the fly for, but Dolly will not drive one of those unless it's an absolute emergency, no matter my confidence that I can work around that. I haven't done it on the fly before, in a real police situation, but I've done it stationary, just me and the car and the connection.

It isn't that Dolly doesn't trust me; she doesn't trust the machines. Or not the hackable ones. She trusts her left arm, for instance. It isn't connected to the internet, or connectable to the internet, and she knows that it isn't. If it was, she would've gone with a more obvious prosthetic, just for the security. Like how she always uses analog guns.

Bristol is interesting, because she can appreciate the need for security most of the time. She trusts me, us, most on *device* security, and lets me scan and tinker with her devices as needed. I think she realizes that I'm already on the honor system with regards to reading her stuff, and has never even tried to swear me to secrecy. Either she has to trust me, or she can't trust me, and she made her decision I guess. We wouldn't be a team if she didn't trust me, and Dolly, implicitly.

Trust is a funny thing. If you'd asked me a few years ago who the people I trusted most in the world were, a socialite and an ex super soldier were not the list. Before I left home, it was my family that I trusted the most, and I didn't leave because we had a falling out, I left because we decided that it was best to split up and spread out so that the government didn't come and pull a Waco on us. Well, Waco wouldn't be right, we weren't a cult or a religious institution, we were a family minding our own business and being as off the grid as possible while also separately still tapped into shortwave radio and satellite internet. I guess Ruby Ridge might be a better comparison. There've been others, of course, because there are always other stories like that. It's not something I talk about much, my upbringing, and I think with separation, some of my family has grown more paranoid than others. We check in every once in a while, via throwaway emails and dead end websites, and message boards for innocuous niche topics. But never for very long; not long enough that somebody with a podcast could put the pieces together.

It would be funny, if one of my brothers was on one of the other teams, but that would be too much of a coincidence, and also too splashy of an event. None of them would ever do something like this, and probably would've tried to discourage me from doing it. But, I always have to have my projects, and right now, this is it. It seemed fun enough and lucrative enough, and Dolly's always up for a road trip. Bristol turns up her nose at some things, but she's also always looking for new experiences to further calibrate her social intelligence. It's like how she first met Dolly in a bottom-rung bar; she wasn't there for fun or because she thought she'd like it, she was there to educate herself.

That's a thing that I really respect about Bristol, she knows her strengths and works for potentials. The only time I've ever seen her even a little off balance was when her old friend Lorraine showed up when we were doing the fake engagement job. Well okay twice, but anybody'll be off balance when they drink a cocktail spiked with ketamine, you can't plan and educate yourself around that. I don't think you can even acclimate yourself to it, like cyanide or whatever. Arsenic? Maybe there's a few things.

Bristol comes back with some shopping bags and Dolly pops the trunk without comment. Dolly also stops at the next convenience store without comment and says "If we're going to Death Valley we need to bring water." She goes inside for seven minutes, and comes out with two flats of bottled water.

"Do you think that will be quite enough?" Bristol asks.

"Probably, but it's better to have too much than too little, right?" Dolly winks at me as she slides the water into the footwell I'm not using in the back seat. "Hey Bitsy, lemme know when we get to one of these that somebody else has done already."

"We haven't yet," I say. "But I'll keep that in mind." She's got sabotage on her mind, which makes sense. We don't know any of the behind the scenes details, how closely they're monitoring anything. If and how they would interrupt, if somebody decided to pull something. I wasn't thinking about a double cross; I'm glad she is. Really, we should always be thinking about a double cross. So few jobs go totally straight.

"We'll have to soon, won't we?" Bristol asks. "How many more of these can there possibly be?"

"We all started at different locations and had different first clues," I say, and then Dolly interrupts and says,

"You're the one who likes logic puzzles, Bristles."

Bristol bites off whatever she was going to say, and then in a brighter tone says "I think Dolly assumes I need to keep occupied, Bits. How many other teams are there? Did you end up finding out?"

"It's ten," I say.

"I didn't *say* you needed to keep occupied," Dolly said. "You just seem to like it best when you have a job."

"Mmm," Bristol says, and I can picture the look on her face, one of her stock masks of serene tolerance.

"How many of 'em do you think are familiar with bullriding?"

"It's an easily searchable phrase," I say, shrugging even though neither of them is looking at me.

"Seems on the nose, though," Dolly says. Her ecigarette is in her mouth but she's not smoking it and I don't know if it's because she forgot or she's out of the juice or what. She probably isn't out.

"Are you suggesting we're being sabotaged? Or sabotaged already? By somebody somehow familiar with our past escapades?" Bristol asks. I can't tell if she thinks Dolly's being ridiculous or not.

Dolly's the one who shrugs. "I'm saying it's possible. Because when they planned the game, it's not like they even knew that you were going to sign up, right Bitsy?"

"That's true, they didn't," I say. Is Dolly being paranoid or is this reasonable caution? I pretty much never think that somebody's suspicions are paranoia. It isn't paranoia if somebody's really after you. "So either it's a coincidence, or a team actually did get that clue ahead of time, and left us this one as a fake."

We drive in silence for a little while. "I think it's ridiculous to be so worried," Bristol says. "The worst case scenario in this instance is that we lose some time, I suppose. It isn't as though Death Valley is uninhabited and unnavigable, after all. And if you're really so concerned, you can simply call the gamerunners. Or I could, since I have the private cell for one of them."

"Nah, don't do that yet. It's probably fine. You just know how trains of thoughts go."

"Many people's, yes. Yours, Dolly darling, almost never."

"Perfect." Dolly looks at me in the rear view mirror and winks.

FINDING THE MECHANICAL bull isn't hard; there's even a hotel here called The Ranch. It all seems very easy but also how hard can the clues be? Somebody comes out from the front of the place when we park near the bull, carrying a remote key fob and an envelope. They've got a game lanyard around their neck with a name tag hunt on it that reads Liam.

"I need you to show your group tag before I turn on the bull," they say.

"I've got it here," I say, and they scrutinize their phone screen for a minute.

"Good, okay," they say, and click a button on their fob.

"We aren't your first group, are we?" Bristol asks. She's wearing both sunglasses and a hat with a broad droopy brim, and they look at her like she's got to be a movie star

"Well I'm not really supposed to say..." they trail off as Dolly takes stuff out of her pockets, depositing it in the driver's seat of the car. Then she stretches until her back cracks, looking at the bull, and picks up a handful of desert sand driveway, rubbing it between her palms.

"Neither of you want to do this, right?" She asks, pausing suddenly. Bristol wrinkles her nose, just a tiny little bit

"No, thank you. I'm quite satisfied to leave it to somebody more practiced."

Dolly nods. "Bits?"

"Also no. I'd never deprive you of the opportunity."

"Fair enough, I didn't want to hog it without even thinking about it." I'm not sure how many bars Dolly has gone to with mechanical bulls, even before we spent time on a bona fide (former) bull rider's ranch, but the number is more than zero.

"You're not. Just be careful "

"You two worry so much," she says, never mind that she's the one who introduced the idea that another team is sabotaging us already or intends to.

At a glance, the mechanical bull is completely normal. The thing that powers it is even normal, not remotely operated or anything like that. The keyfob was to unlock a protective housing that had been put over the controls, I guess for added security. On closer inspection, it isn't just set up in the middle of a dirt parking lot, the immediate surroundings are foam that were painted to blend in.

"This isn't at the hotel all the time, is it?" I ask Liam and they give a slightly nervous laugh.

"Oh no, not at all. This is just for the game. I'm also not a hotel employee, I was hired by the gamerunners."

"That makes sense." I look back down at my phone, because it's a more normal gesture than staring straight ahead at my HUD to see the things I'm keeping track of, my messages, our timer in the game, where the other players are. It would be interesting to know where the gamerunners also are, and where the mainframe is, since they're clearly using it remotely. My progress bar on that is full but I'm still not in yet.

"Did they call you Bits?" Liam asks hesitantly, and I blink and look up at them, remembering hazily the way that Null acted when we met, and how Dolly crowed about how I was famous and didn't even know it. I guess it makes sense, that my name would be known; I can think of a couple of other famous and/or notorious hackers, even people I've messaged with occasionally.

"Yeah, I'm Bits."

They look around a little, but it's just Bristol and Dolly and I out here, and Bristol and Dolly are talking just slightly out of earshot at the mechanical bull. I can't imagine what they're talking about, Dolly could've been done by now. Liam leans in a little and says "I'm Smog."

For a second I think oh no, I'm not going to know this person's handle, but my brain fast cycles and it clicks. They did a credit card/crypto hack a few years back. "Hey! Nice to meet you. That was a good job."

"Thank you." They also were afraid, I think, that I wouldn't know who they were, but they stand up a little straighter with the praise. "If you need any help with this, I could..."

"Oh, no, that's okay. Thank you I mean. But we want to do it fair and square, this is just for fun." Is it rude bragging, to say playing a game with prizes like that is just for fun? Bristol would be able to tell me. "Dolly is very enthusiastic"

"I can see that," Smog says, with something like wonderment.

Bristol backs off, shaking her head, and Dolly gets up on the bull and gets herself settled before giving the thumbs up, leaving her left hand in the air and holding on with her right. Smog gives a nod, then reaches down and hits the switch, and there's a brief pause and then the bull grinds to life. I can only assume the desert environment isn't super great for it, and it's been out here for a couple of days at least, as the gamerunners got everything set up.

I remember Dolly once telling me that there's only so many patterns that mechanical bulls have, and that a lot of the ones she's ridden have started out with the 'head down' buck and spin, and that's what this one does. I don't think I ever asked Dolly how many mechanical bulls she's ridden; the number's more than zero, and so that's already more than I've experienced. The control panel has a running digital counter, and as the bull bucks and spins, and then changes direction, Dolly stays on, stays upright even, though I can almost hear her teeth clack together during one of the direction changes. She gives a whoop when it hits eight seconds. I don't know how she knows it was eight seconds. Smog hits the button again and the bull settles down into its hibernation mode again and Dolly slides off.

"Piece of cake," she says, breathing a little hard, but not too much, and Bristol claps.

"Brilliant performance, darling."

"I've ridden that model before, if not that specific bull. I think there's only so many of 'em, y'know?" She looks over at Smog and me. "So we got the next clue?"

Smog gives kind of a start and fumbles with the envelope they've been holding all along. "Sorry, sorry, here."

Dolly briefly gives me a short eyebrows-raised 'what's with them?' sort of look and I shrug. "Thanks Smog, we appreciate it," I say.

"You're welcome. Good luck! I think you're doing pretty good, right? I think you have—no you wouldn't know, I shouldn't say."

"Nope," I say with a smile, and Dolly laughs.

"No cheating!" she says.

"Is it really cheating?" Bristol asks. Smog looks at the three of us, just unprepared to handle the reality of us, I guess. I wonder what they know about us, or think they know about us. But they've got intel on all the teams, are they going to be like this for all of them?

"I don't think it's cheating to tell us if we're in the lead or not," I say after a pause. "It wouldn't be able to affect our performance, right?"

"That's right," Smog says. "You're in the lead, and the next team after you needs one more to tie."

"Which means we gotta get going, right?" Dolly asks. "We have the clue?" I raise the envelope. "Perfect. Hey, thanks a lot!"

"You're welcome," Smog says. "Good luck!"

"Thanks," I say, and we go back to the car.

"What's the clue, Bitsy?" Dolly asks, checking her mirrors as she backs out, eyeing the charge on the car.

"I didn't look yet, hold on." I open the envelope, plain manilla like the other ones. I pull out the index card and read the careful lettering. "From Sea to Shining Sea."

Silence in the car, and then Dolly laughs. "What the fuck does that mean?"

"I don't know." I search it, and it's a line from a really old patriotic song. Okay. "Bristol?"

"Yeah, Bristles, culture us? It's obvious a certain kinda guy is the one making these clues, maybe the same one who gave you his number. He knew you were snooty, and wants to woo you with obscure shit."

"I am not *snooty*," Bristol says with a little sniff, and then laughs. "Oh dear that sounded very snooty."

"Point," Dolly says.

I click through a few things, half listening to them. Patriotic song lyrics referencing what? Cool, great, Manifest Destiny. Okay but also referenced in stuff about the transcontinental railroad, which went through Sacramento and eventually was finished up in San Francisco. But Stanford is where there's a museum that has the golden spike (one of the golden spikes?) that they drove when the building effort from the east coming west and the building effort from the west going east met. "They wouldn't want us to steal that, right? That would be weird." I look up, and Dolly looks at me in the mirror and Bristol has turned around halfway in her seat to look over her shoulder at me.

"Gotta tell us the rest of the thought, Bitsy."

"The golden spike from the transcontinental railroad is in a museum at Stanford. Well, one of them. There's also one in a museum in San Francisco."

"I imagine they don't want us to steal anything," Bristol says. "This isn't a scavenger hunt, it's a puzzle game."

"You're right, this is just the first thing that's come up that seemed really like, mobile."

"Well and there's only the one in the world, so you probably assumed Bristol'd want it for her very own, to keep with that egg or something. Make a li'l shadowbox."

"I guess they made four?"

"Four egg shadowboxes?" Dolly's grinning, and Bristol sighs.

"Four golden spikes," I say.

"Even better, that's one for each of us and then one that the museum can keep."

"I do not want a golden railroad spike, personally, but thank you," Bristol says.

"More for us," Dolly says. "So...Stanford?"

"I guess? I don't know if one makes more sense than the other."

"I dunno. Is one on the way to the other?"

"No but yes. Stanford's first, if we do this route." I send it to her GPS.

"I'd just like to leave Death Valley, please," Bristol says.

"You just object to the name, Bristles, look at all the natural splendor around us. How can you love Morocco and not Death Valley? Is it just the PR or what? You're smarter'n that."

I expect Bristol to have a sharp or even huffy comeback, and instead there's thoughtful silence. "You know, maybe you're right," she says after a few minutes, as we drive through one of the areas that's carpeted with wildflowers. There's a superbloom this year, is what sites said when I'd searched the flowers. Whatever a superbloom is. Well I mean, we're looking at it. "It is very lovely, it just has a bad name."

"There, see. Not so bad?"

"No, not so bad."

"Good, now I can give you the bad news," Dolly says and Bristol sighs.

"Oh goodness. What is it?"

"It's like eight hours to Stanford and we gotta stop at least once to charge."

"It isn't as though I'm disused to travel, Dolly darling."

"Well there, good, she took it better than I thought," Dolly says to me.

"Yeah, she took it really well."

Bristol laughs. "You two are ridiculous."

"That's us!" Dolly agrees, taking out her ecigarette.

Chapter Seven

Of course, the museum where the golden spike is also happens to be at Stanford University, which isn't like, where the internet started per se (that was ARPANET at UCLA), but it received the first internet message, so the story goes, and was a hotbed for early internet culture. A lot of slang that gets used among hackers is still Stanford stuff, even though some things are so many times removed that it just doesn't make any sense anymore. Like talking about dialing a phone when the last rotary anything was manufactured more than a hundred years ago. So it makes me wonder what else we might have access to, once we're on the campus. What's still online? What's laying around, disused, in storage rooms? I'll keep an eye out for student credentials and how they work, for future exploration.

There's also a history of computing museum at Stanford. Or there are exhibits throughout the computer sciences building? I didn't take the time to really look at first, because of the job at hand, but now I do. There's both, now, a museum and also things in the computer sciences buildings, because there are also more than one now.

We're almost to Stanford when I sit up in the back seat and paw the headset off my face. "This is too easy."

"What now?" Dolly asks, in a tone that says my sudden movement behind her flipped all the 'time for violence already?' switches that she's got. To her credit, she only swerved a little bit and corrected immediately.

"We aren't perfect trivia puzzle riddle solvers, this has been too easy." God damn it, I should've been the one to sign us up, so I could look those people in the face. Not that I don't think Bristol can't do a logic puzzle, that isn't it. "Like the hardest thing is how many times we've had to drive like, eight hours. And also the bull thing I guess."

"The bull thing," Dolly repeats, laughing a little.

"Bits, darling, this game was your idea. Why would you suddenly mistrust it so?" Bristol turns to look at me, and there is real concern in her face. Whether it's concern about my concern, or whether she's worried that I've got something wrong with me, I can't tell.

"Well I'm not sure I ever trust anything entirely," I say. "But I don't have proof I guess. It's just a feeling." I pull my headset up for a second, check my HUD. "Oh and I'm still not in their mainframe yet, that's something. That's been bothering me."

"Well just try Will's agency credentials and see," Dolly says in a hard-edged, fake cheerful voice that says she's fine with this turning more serious than our little family road trip.

"They wouldn't leave anything that was on that laptop active," I say.

"Mmmhmm?" Bristol isn't even sure what to ask.

"Okay yeah I wrote a program to use everything on Will's laptop to see if they left a channel still open to try and trap me."

"That's our girl," Dolly says.

As I'm pulling my headset on again, Bristol says "Girls, aren't we being the teensiest bit paranoid? You said there are other teams and you can see their movements. That would be a *very* elaborate trap just for us."

"Ain't paranoia if somebody's really after you," Dolly says. "Which we know they are."

"Yes, but—"

I think of Smog back in Death Valley, knowing who I was, and try to compare it against Null knowing who I was, back when we were getting Bristol out of custody, but I can't make it match up right. My mental video from that time isn't really reliable. It makes sense for a hacker helping in a real life puzzle game to know who I am; it makes equivalent sense for a government agent inserting into a real life puzzle game to have been briefed on who I am. Who we all are.

My mainframe hack is at the same percent which means either their security is that good, which it can be, we're all hackers here, or they've got a countermeasure stalling it, and I cut that connection. I should've thought of this sooner but I was familiar with previous games of varying sizes and there were no red flags. Maybe this is paranoia but I think in this business paranoia pays. Especially if we're merrily driving around in the U.S. knowing damn well that there's at least one unnamed government agency that wants its hands on us.

In VR, nobody else is around the mainframe that I can see. They've made it look like a casino building, flat-topped and round, all flashing lights running around it in a pattern. I set a program recording and parsing the pattern because there have been dumber things than people putting the key right there on the outside of the thing that's locked, physically and virtually. Sometimes people think a physically locked thing is very secure, but I've seen Dolly open a hotel room keypad safe with a spoon, so security is an eternally variable thing.

I circle around it, look at the different angles and potentials. I sort through the credentials that I skimmed not from Will's laptop, but from the connection that I used it to follow back to the Agency, in as subtle and thorough a smash and grab as I was able to perform before he called it in and access was pulled. Which was a very successful smash and grab, actually, as I've been able to spoof other agents' connections when I wanted to have a little walk through every once in a while, to try and see if they'd pinged us lately or added to our files. When Dolly returned that laptop to Will, she said that he about dropped dead the second he saw her. I know that level of intimidation was part of her goal, even as keeping him sympathetic and intrigued is part of Bristol's.

This doesn't appear to be an Agency mainframe, though, as nothing matches up. Maybe they're independent contractors, there are any number of bounties for us and other hackers who would've been drawn in by the promise of challenge and reward. Or maybe they are just who they say they are, their own team of hackers having some fun. Is anybody who they say they are? It's hard to tell. Bristol absolutely tells you who she is, if you're paying attention. Dolly too. And I mostly try to say nothing at all.

My program pings me, tells me that there is deliberately not a pattern in the lights pattern, which means it's absolutely a security thing, just like the wall of lava lamps that's been at a particular encryption company for decades now, and I wonder briefly about how long an individual lava lamp will keep functioning. No wonder my auto hack stalled out.

Thing thing about security is that the flaw is nearly always human. A potential vulnerability here is one that I already thought about; the geotags. They should've thought of it, these things absolutely shouldn't create a vulnerability to the mainframe if they indeed go back to it and not just a dedicated laptop or whatever, but bigger things have been brought down by less, historically.

I sort through the lines of code I have around me, find the geotag for the Fashion Police, and yup, follow it right to the mainframe, and into the mainframe. There's a partition for these so okay, that's smart. But there's only so many ways to partition access like this, and I think of Dolly with the spoon again, as I feel out the edges, metaphorically but also literally via code, and I do find a vulnerability. If this was a real room that the geotags all connected to, what I find is essentially the wire that connects from the other side of the wall and leads to the rest of the building. That's probably a bad metaphor, but that's how I picture it. Phone cords and motel rooms.

The concept of the mainframe is maybe an antiquated one, or maybe it's just audacious now, *extravagant*, to think of using a physically large computer for large computing things, when computing has gotten *so* small and portable. They put men on the moon with less computing power than Dolly's vintage robot dog, and now I'm in VR using something that fits into what is to all appearances a toy. You can buy low-grade VR headsets in line at the grocery store and play a bunch of built-in games, or walk through a bunch of premade experiences, for fifty bucks. Mine cost more than fifty bucks, but I think my point is clear.

The mainframe here, that I'm referring to, is a big computational machine. I think physically large, in addition to being powerful, which again makes me think this is an agency project. Do the gamerunners know? Do they just think they're using generous corporate sponsorship for computational power, and that's the shell the agency is using? Questions for later, I need to figure out the goal here.

Slowly, carefully, I move through the data, look at the geotags, scan electronic signatures. I'm not super worried about being detected; at my level, I've spent years creeping around people's data architecture not touching anything and most of them have never known. Targets large and small, because sometimes you get curious.

I copy stuff as I go, that I think might be of interest, but I keep going because I want to know who the owner of the mainframe is. I don't have proof yet that it isn't the gamerunners, I just have that feeling that it isn't. Their tech startup wouldn't have a thing like this, they're clustering laptops and phones and headsets. Again, they could've leased computing power, but why do it for a silly thing like this? It doesn't add up, unless this is a rich kid with access to their parent's company or something like that. That's the most innocuous flight of fancy I can take, I think. Maybe I'll come up with more later.

It's isn't unusual, that they've got it set up so I need to be deeper in the data architecture to find ownership. Hanging your name out front can make you a target, for attacks serious and recreational. Arguably it's also a trap, but since they're already tracking us as game participants both via the phones and the geotags that they gave us, they don't really have much to gain by knowing who I am and that I'm here. And of course I'm proud of my own security, but if it goes untested, it gets static and stale. Then I get too lazy and full of myself.

On cue, I get one of my own security popups. I'm not securing a whole mainframe, so it's perfectly reasonable for me to have several layers of security. Ablative, almost. I think Dolly would appreciate that I know that word. And, for instance, I know that our dragonscale armor *isn't* ablative, but that some of the heavier stuff she has is. Though speaking of dragonscale...

//We should swap to riot gear when we get the chance// I text Dolly. She can handle bickering with Bristol about it.

//ten four// Dolly says, maybe a little too quickly. Did we park? I'm not in full VR immersion but I'm also not paying attention to my physicality. It isn't a good plan to split my attention right now.

The attempt at breaching my security was barely an attack, just a packet ping that my systems rebuffed. It might even just be an auto-response to my connection, but it's sure to draw a human response, and I set a stopwatch running for fun to see how long it takes before we make contact, and I stop being such a tourist and get to more serious business. Really, they should've assumed I'd do this, maybe they just thought it would be way earlier in the game.

Though that reminds me, while I can take advantage of the mainframe power, I do a scan of the other team's geotags, and then search for nearby vulnerable cameras. Traffic cameras, Rings, whatever, I don't care. Are the other teams real, or are they digital packets to make me think we're playing a real game? Is that why the game is *so* widespread, so it makes sense that we wouldn't run into other teams right away, and not wonder about it until it's too late? But what's the too late here, what's *their* endgame? They could've swooped in with black helicopters when Smog had eyes on us in Death Valley, if capture is the goal.

My security pings me again, then a second and third time quickly. Not human yet, though, stopwatch still counting up. I get to what I assume is the ownership credentials that I'm looking for and of course there's more passive security here as well, it'd be laughable if there wasn't but I'm getting antsy. I know this is low risk but also my alarm bells are going off even assuming what I'm assuming. Maybe I'm just making things out to be worse than they really are.

But I run my utility of the Agency credentials that I've gleaned and by its very nature I don't know *which* one unlocks the files for to grab, but one of them does and then in my HUD I get confirmation that I can have eyes on just one other team and isn't that interesting. I take a screenshot, then break the connection with my stopwatch still counting upwards, and then power down, just in case something did get in under my radar. I sit up, pulling my headset down so it hangs around my neck.

We're parked on the side of the road, Dolly and Bristol both turned around to look at me. Nobody else seems to be here, no other cars are around us.

"I don't really know how yet," I say. "But this is probably a trap."

Chapter Eight

"Okay, so let's get this straight," Dolly says, another thirty or so miles down the road, when we're all sitting around a table at a diner, eyeing the holo menus. "The new working theory here is that the agency is running this shindig and there's really only one other team? They spoofed the rest of it, right down to the gamerunners?"

"Well those guys could be in the agency and just nobody knows," I say. "Or they could've been strongarmed into it as part of a deal. That's the theory I'm betting on, actually, since we know the agency makes deals." I look at Bristol, who smiles briefly. If this was an anime, she'd have just one single sharp tooth bared for that fleeting second.

"But, darlings, if the game is a ruse, then what is the goal? Why such a farce?"

"Well I don't know yet," I say, and the waitress comes by right then. I blink at the menu some more because I haven't thought about food in hours, as in, it hasn't occurred to me that I might want food. Because why not one team but two? Why actually set up clues in locations? What benefit could come from fooling multiple groups of people like this? And there's no way to trust the payout now, the winner isn't getting all of those prizes. There's no reason to expect them to honor—oh the waitress. I look up and she's gone again, and I look at Dolly.

"I got you chicken fingers and fries," she says with a laugh. "It seemed like a burger might take too much processing power right now."

"Thanks." I blink some more but she's right. Bristol now has a tiny wine bottle and what must pass for a wine glass in this place. I can't keep track of what kinds of diners you can expect to be able to drink at and what ones you can't. I look out the window and it's actually later than I would've thought. I have connection to clocks of course but what is time. "Okay I guess they must never have intended for anybody to find out that this is anything but a game?"

"So they're really ponying up all that cash and stuff?" Dolly's eyebrows show me just how doubtful she is.

"I don't know. It seems impossible, right? But that would be on the gamerunners, and tarnish their reputation in the community. So maybe that's just doing double duty for them." A narrative is starting to form for me, and I don't know how right it is, but it *feels* right. "Okay, let's say the agency caught the gamerunners doing something, what it is doesn't matter. Caught, interrogated, got to the 'let's make a deal' portion. The agency needs access to something that they can't legitimately request or access, and their people can't handle it. Maybe the gamerunners can't either, and that was part of their initial plan."

"So they need more people with particular skills to do the job," Bristol says. She doesn't look too pleased with her wine, once she sips it, but I know she likes having a prop in her hand.

"Exactly. So they lured us and the other team in with the promise of the game, and they set up the game for real, so that we wouldn't know anything weird was going on."

"It'd be funny if they still made those nerds do most of the work," Dolly says, leaning back for her burger to get set in front of her.

I laugh, surprised. "I guess they'd have to, right? Other than pointing us to a particular geographic location."

"Do you think Stanford has whatever prize they're after?" Bristol asks. Now she's eyeing her food dubiously. We already knew that the roadside diner experience is not what Bristol is into, it's a wonder she agreed to this at all. I think it all looks okay, but my food opinions and Bristol's don't always match up. Don't ever match up, from her perspective.

"Maybe, but I'd be surprised if we get to the endgame so soon. Even though I'd love to just spend a month at Stanford, probably."

"How come?" Dolly mumbles with her mouth full.

"Computer history stuff. Internet history stuff." I shrug. "Nerd stuff."

"Figures."

"Should we try to contact the other group?" Bristol asks. "To see if they've noticed anything?"

"Bristles, that's real sportin' of you, wanting to compare notes with the competition."

"While it might benefit us to keep them in the dark, it is worth inquiring if they know anything, wouldn't you say? Are they very near to us?"

"No, they're still in Nevada." From the data I skimmed, none of their clues so far had any overlap with ours.

"Maybe it's not a trap," Dolly says. "Maybe it's recruitment."

"That's still a trap," Bristol says, making a little face.

"Tomato, tomahto," Dolly says, finishing her burger. "Some people never had the chance to go legit and would jump at it if they could."

"I do suppose that's true." Bristol looks at me. "Have you seen any indication of that?"

"Of what, that this game by these gamerunners could be a government agency recruitment tool?"

"Don't make it sound so silly, darling."

"I'm not, I'm making sure I've got it straight." They wait, and while I think about it I run a search, but nothing comes up. "No, they always seemed legit. Not legit. Or I mean, not government plants. So either it's recent or it's how they've always been, but on the face, nothing has changed, nobody's seen any red flags or raised alarms. Unless I'm in the wrong whisper networks, which is always possible."

"Whisper networks?" Dolly has her ecigarette on the table in front of her, but seemed to remember just in time that she couldn't do that in here, and she's lightly tapping it against the tabletop, end to end, while we wait for Bristol to finish eating, and to pay. Or maybe they already paid and I was distracted.

"Yeah, like. Backchannels to warn people about stuff when it isn't necessarily safe to just broadcast it." Bristol nods; Bristol knows.

"Gotcha," Dolly says. Maybe she's less mystified or maybe she's just never heard it called that. "Okay, we ready to roll? That golden spike isn't gonna drive itself."

"We aren't—" I start, and she laughs.

"I know, I know."

Bristol folds her napkin, and we go out to the parking lot, where in the street lights we see that the car has a flat tire. Dolly crouches to examine it, vapor trailing above her head. It isn't completely flat, not a rubber puddle surrounding the rim, but it's at-a-glance obvious.

"Did we pick up a nail?" I ask, and she shrugs.

"Hard to say. Doesn't look like a knife, anyway," she says cheerfully. "Or a screwdriver."

"Were you expecting sabotage?" Bristol asks, eyebrows raised.

"Yeah, always. I'm surprised you're not." Dolly stands back up again and goes to trunk, feels around for the mechanism. "One reason I like jeep-shaped things, they hang the spare on the outside."

"Does this even have a spare?" I ask, leaning inside and popping the trunk. Some cars have a voice activated password for that. There has to still be a physical mechanism, right? Maybe not.

"Well it's got a donut and I put a full sized one in here too. Besides having a patch kit, of course."

"Of course," Bristol says. I'm not certain she knows what a donut is, in this context. I don't think I would, with her background.

Dolly pulls a little jack out, hands it to me. "You can handle that, right Bitsy?"

"Sure." In a bigger vehicle no, I'd have no idea where to put the jack. The bumper? With this car, though, I know I can put it in the space between the doors and that'll lift it up the right way. I crank the crank, and the car lifts up enough that the tire hangs straight again, and then so it's high enough that Dolly can pull it off and trade it out. I don't see a screw or anything from my vantage, or other obvious punctures. And the other team that I *know* is a live team isn't anywhere near us, so sabotage wouldn't have anything to do with them. It doesn't have to mean anything. Is this the first flat I've changed with Dolly? I think so. Statistically, it was bound to happen.

"I've somehow never done this before," Bristol says, watching us work.

"Will you be insulted if I say I'm not surprised?" Dolly asks, spinning the tire iron on the bolts. When she gets the tire off she rolls it in the light, examining the surface. "Here, look, this big chunk of metal got in it. Just something off a truck or something, probably, that was in the road." She wiggles it out and drops it at our feet. "Or maybe it's off one of those thingers the police drop in a car chase. Hole might be too big for the patch, but it can cure in the trunk."

I'm a little surprised when Bristol crouches and picks up the piece of metal; she doesn't typically volunteer to touch dirty things, or anonymous sharp things. "It *does* seem innocuous," she says thoughtfully, looking from it to the other cars in the lot. At least a couple left after we got here, but they were just normal-seeming diners, that I could tell. Normal civilian devices and vehicles.

"But now you don't think so? Uh-oh, Bitsy, nothing's more dangerous than a new conspiracy head." Dolly's letting the jack down again already, the new tire screwed on snug.

"We are well aware of the existence of the agency," Bristol says primly. "It's hardly a flight of fancy to suspect them, once we've already started suspecting them."

"Yeah, if the shoe fits." Dolly checks the patch, then tosses everything back in the trunk and slams it. "This is what we get for thinking we'll profit off of a little fun."

"Dolly, you always have fun."

She grins at me. "Well, yeah. But you two don't."

"Point."

"I don't know what you girls are talking about, I find our work highly amusing." She pauses, perhaps running a couple of historic mishaps through her head. "I typically find our work highly amusing."

"That's the spirit. Bitsy, does this change our plans at all?"

The ten million dollar question. "No, I guess it doesn't. We don't know anything, so we don't have anything to go on."

"And if we ditch now, we'll never find out," Dolly says, once we're all in the car.

"We simply must find out," Bristol says. "Either we genuinely are so skilled that we've outsmarted the gamerunners and will tidily win, or it is the agency again, and we'll know what measures to take next."

"Leavin' the country's always a nice start," Dolly says, and Bristol sort of hums in response. I know it's been a while since she's been back to Morocco, and also that she doesn't consider that location burned for some reason.

No, I know the reason; she considers Will to be on the hook already, if not outright compromised. I think he's compromised, but he doesn't know it yet, which makes him still dangerous. But Bristol makes survival decisions first, so her decisions regarding him have been shrewd and airtight, even when taking the occasional risk. Whomst among us doesn't take the occasional risk? Deciding to do the game was a risk. Being in the States at all is a risk. Some days, breathing is a risk, it's just how it is.

That sounds dramatic, but it isn't. When you're wanted by unspecified shadow government agency or agencies, it's easy to want to go far far away and hole up somewhere. When you learn that that agency or agencies operate across international borders, even in limited capacity, well. You might get tired of waiting to get caught and just keep living your life instead.

Assuming agency involvement, there's a few reasons for two live teams instead of one. In case one of us fails, the other can still get whatever target the agency won't go after themselves. Or they want to reassure us that we aren't a target and that the game is real, with multiple teams. Or we're the bait, to lure in the other team and assure *them* that this is all on the up and up.

I worry it in circles long enough that it becomes impossible to worry about in a tangible way. It's either too big for us to affect or the things we would do to affect it are the things we'd do anyway as standard operating procedure. We just know to be on our guard now, which we typically are anyway. I think Dolly most out of all of us, but maybe I'm wrong. By her very nature, Bristol is hard to get a read on, other than how she wants you to perceive her.

The other live team isn't as diversified as we are, they're mostly hackers and one gearhead, if I'm remembering right. Cars and motorcycles and anything with an engine, really. That might be my in with them, now that I think about it. I pull up a recent article on the 3D printed helicopters that Dolly's friend Butler and his business partners were making and marketing, and then root around for a public source of contact information for the gearhead, who's listed in the game signup as "Cortina" and that makes me wonder if he is a she or a they maybe and I genuinely don't know, but I trace that name to a forum post that seems like something I could've stumbled across and send off the message.

I get an almost immediate response. It's almost funny how fast it is, but I'd probably do the same thing, if an internet big deal suddenly messaged me out of nowhere, and I didn't know they knew I existed. Well. If I worried about things like that, it's kind of confusing to think about. I can't be responsible for how people think of me; I can only be responsible for the things that I do.

//Is this real?// is all the message says, and I wonder over it a little bit like. Which part? That it's from me, or that the helicopters are 3D printed.

//Yeah, almost like any other helicopter// I send back. //Lighter weight, maybe a shorter range.//

//No, I mean is this really Bits. Sorry, in a situation right now.//

//Sorry. Yes, it's really Bits.// There's a long pause, and I can only imagine they're all conferring with one another. //You're in the game, right?//

//.....yes?//

//I'm not trying to cheat or get answers from you or anything, just wanted to give you a wave and make sure things were going okay. We just got a flat tire so I was killing time.//

//Bad luck. Things are good, are we supposed to even have contact?//

//Probably not.//

"They don't seem to think anything is weird but me reaching out," I say to the front seat.

"They meanin' the other team?"

"Yeah."

"Perhaps they're safe then, at least," Bristol says.

"Very magnanimous of you, Bristles," Dolly says. "We can imagine you have a heart."

Bristol gives a sniff but lets that ride. "Should I call Ant?"

"Who now?" Dolly asks.

"The gamerunner who gave her his number."

"Fuck, I forgot about that. So many men felled wherever she goes..."

"Now who's dramatic," Bristol sighs, but I can hear her smile.

"Well is he cute?"

"By whose standards, darling?" Dolly shrugs. "And am I calling him or not?"

"To be a super spy and get him to spill the game's secrets to you? Didn't you need more relationship-buildin' to get to that stage of wrapped around your finger?"

"Relationship building, like...texting throughout the game?" Bristol asks sweetly.

"Sure, like that." Dolly gives her a suspicious glance. "You holdin' out on us?"

"Perhaps I am."

"Bitsy, did you know about this?"

"Given the constant stream of contacts that Bristol gets at all time of the day and night, no, it's not my business unless she makes it my business or we're looking out for something in particular. Bristol, did you really?"

"I did, yes."

"So it'd be weird if you suddenly called him instead, huh?"

"I do think it would, which wouldn't *particularly* bother me, but you know how these things go."

"Yeah, sure," Dolly says, in a tone that means she absolutely does not.

"No, I get it," I say. "Especially if you haven't been talking about the game."

Bristol laughs. "We absolutely have not been, why would we."

"Why would you," Dolly repeats, a laugh in her voice but not laughing. "*Obviously.*"

"What have you been talking about?" I ask.

"Oh, nothing terribly important, darling, just getting to know you chitchat. He hasn't traveled much and would love to do more, so I recommended him the best credit card for the rewards points to interest ratio."

"You did what?" Dolly says.

"Is it really so odd?"

"I guess not." Dolly laughs, looks at me. "So, keep on target?"

"Keep on target," I say.

Chapter Nine

The Stanford campus is like a city within a city. It's weird, how little time I've spent on college campuses, any of them. I think it'd be easy to blend, and I'm keeping that as a back pocket solution for the next time I or we need to immediately hide out from prying eyes. Dolly parks by the museum and I look at the cars around us to see how the parking credentials works. Students have etags of course, more temporary visitors have holos for their windows with a little addition to their car code, and museum visitors just need to feed the meter.

Quick quiz, how do the three of us deal with parking meters?

Bristol enjoys the esoteria of coins, and even though most people don't carry cash modernly, and especially not coins, she does. Though Bristol also hardly drives herself anywhere, and even more rarely has to deal with something like a parking meter.

Dolly lies to them with a paperclip. Why paperclips are still an item that exist in the world and are manufactured every year is not a question for me to ask; some industries are still paper-driven. Some countries, too. She has other tools she can use too, but paperclips are small, and flex right but have the right stiffness.

For me, it depends on the meters. Some are genuine antiques, only mechanical, and I'll pay them in coins or slugs, whatever the detritus in my pockets gives me. I can do the paperclip thing, or I can also use other tools. If it's an internet device, I can fool it with a magnet or a fake RFID debit card or by hopping onto its network and lying to it.

The museum wouldn't normally be open this late, but there's some kind of additional exhibition opening and reception, and there are enough people around that it's clear school is also in session. Unless they're all just here for the special event. I have kind of a funny thought, that at least we're not actually racing nine other teams now or whatever, we can just act pretty normal. Visitors are expected here, even if we wouldn't hold up the illusion of being students, since we haven't prepped for that. But the pressure is different. I see Bristol looking at sleekly bearded maybe-professor types, and when I look at Dolly quizzically, she rolls her eyes. Oh, it's that kind of looking. But she's also making eyes at the nearby sculpture garden, that we have to walk past to go into the museum, and that I understand.

Plus, on a job or not, I never went to this many museums and things before I knew Bristol. It just wasn't within the framework of my existence. When museums were mentioned in my childhood, they were described as housing items stolen from their rightful owners and cultures, which is true and not true. The Elgin Marbles, in Europe? Yeah. The Golden Spike, at Stanford? No. But nuance is hard with prepper mindsets.

The statues outside here are interesting, but not fascinating to me, and maybe sometime I'll ask Bristol to recommend some art. She has to have something in mind that she thinks I'd like. That's the kind of thing Bristol seems to do, catalogs things in her head as they relate to people that she might be called upon to interact with. She can talk to anybody about all kinds of things as a result.

We get into the museum, past ionic columns that look weird to me for reasons I can't describe, and Dolly says "Okay, where're we going, Bitsy?" once we're inside and I blink at the marble entry that we're looking at, staircases going up to arches, and then look around for a sign. I step out of the trickle of foot traffic and find a QR code to scan, holding my headset to my face to look at the virtual guest welcome, the map of the museum.

"Well it's not one of the exhibits, it's..." and then I trail off because there are collections and exhibitions and those are two different things so then I just search the spike and it says it's on display but not *where*, like why can't I just select it and have a place on the map light up? Well there's only so big this place is, it'd be in poor form to go tearing into their network because I'm frustrated by visitor UI. Oh it *is* an exhibit, it's just about Stanton and not specifically the *railroad*. I was just asking my question wrong.

I lower my headset and Bristol is earnestly saying to somebody in a suit jacket and a lanyard with a dangling name tag "Oh, she's quite all right, she just gets these *headaches* sometimes, it's the light I think...There, see? No intervention required." They look at me with a small, dubious frown, and look back to Bristol.

"We will be closing soon, but, if you need further assistance—"

"No, no, it's fine. But thank you so much." She doesn't say darling, I add that to my mental catalog. A college student wouldn't say darling, so she doesn't say it to this random campus person. She also didn't change into riot gear; I'd brought it up, but we'd immediately moved on, and she looks exactly as though she belongs here, in her romper dress thing and sandals.

"Ready to roll?" Dolly asks.

"Well I didn't—"

"That's okay, Bristol gathered some information when it seemed to the casual viewer like you were havin' an episode of some kind."

"How would what I just did be so weird on a college campus?" Or anywhere, really. VR having become as ubiquitous as it is, stepping aside to pull your goggles up for a second isn't really so different from walking around looking at your phone.

Dolly shrugs, nodding at Bristol so that we start walking. "Hell if I know."

"Every setting has its own rules," Bristol says, as though it's readily obvious how I broke any social rules.

I know enough program languages that I could write like, a neutral social interactions protocol for myself if I wanted to, with prompts in my HUD. If this, then you can do/say this. I'm not going to, though. Most of the time I don't draw notice, and if I wasn't here with Dolly and Bristol, I wouldn't have done that, not just out in the open. I would've used my HUD or I would've gone to a bathroom or something.

It's another indicator, I guess, that the game isn't a real game. They haven't had wild-eyed weirdoes running in here looking for the golden spike to find the next clue. Everything's business as usual. My focus was elsewhere, but now I can just load my 'how to behave in a museum' program that I didn't write because who needs a program for that?

I follow Bristol and Dolly through the halls, playing the 'where's Dolly's gun hidden?' game, though also I guess it depends on *which* gun because sometimes she's got a really little one that she's trying out and those go up sleeves pretty easily. In addition to the kind of small-but-normal-sized gun she can holster in the small of her back and with riot gear you absolutely can't tell. And because Dolly herself is a weapon, whether she's carrying something additional or not never changes her bearing. She stands up straight enough for Bristol's tastes most of the time, at least.

I was for some reason under the impression that Dolly's gun would be the only one present, but then I glimpse a security guard and his holster. Okay then. I guess mass shootings being what they are, most places opt for armed guards. Were there even metal detectors at the doors? Not that I noticed, and actually with all of the tech so many people carry at all times, just a regular metal detector would have too many false positives, so even if they did have them at one time, they probably had to take them out. You can't have them going off for people's cybernetic limbs and other implants and personal webs of phone-watch-tablet-eye stuff, it's just too much.

The golden spike is behind plexiglass, of course, and then in another separate box of its own. My leap of logic to 'do they expect us to steal it?' didn't make sense, obviously, because that isn't what the game is. But it is what the agency might expect of us, if they thought we might have a buyer, god knows why we would. I'm sure enough people, modernly, are obsessed with the old time railroad days and maybe have the money to be esoteric collectors of the stuff, but even then, most of them wouldn't want something out of an active museum display that they couldn't show off to their other railroad enthusiast friends. Plus there are really good 3D scans of this online, and you could print a reasonable copy for display, just so that you had it aesthetically. Even with the slow rise of high-speed rail in the states, I don't know if anybody's capitalized on that aesthetic, but really that's probably for the better, what with the marginalized labor and all. They don't want to call attention to historic wrongs while perpetuating current ones.

There aren't any paper brochures in the room, and we sort of mill around looking at the exhibit without looking at the exhibit.Well. I'm not really looking at the exhibit, I think it's very possible that Bristol is and equally possible that Dolly isn't. I look at Dolly and she's looking at a set of bull's horns that are mounted on the wall above the door.

I go and look at the spike itself. For something gold driven into the ground, it looks pretty good actually. It has some dings where I assume the hammer hit it, and The Last Spike is engraved on that end. The length of it is also engraved, with names and things, but I could've seen that online in its picture, or by reading the articles about it, coming here wouldn't have been necessary. There's a more normal looking railroad spike tossed in there too, bend near the sharp end, and I wonder if they drove that one first to make room for the ceremonial gold one. It would make sense.

"San Francisco, then?" I ask. This room is painted red on three walls where there aren't exhibit cases, and that bothers me in a way I can't quite put my finger on. The other wall is a big painting, and that's what Bristol is looking at, her head cocked as though somebody's telling a story and she wants them to know that she is listening, enchanted.

"No, darling, I think the clue is where this painting was. There's an odd little video that explains this scene, and then describes how to get to its setting through the campus and nearby buildings."

"Well ain't that something," Dolly says. Now she's looking at the plaster death masks to our right. Bristol looks at her, and then me, and shrugs minutely. I scan the code for the video and watch it myself.

"This is in the virtual tour, though, we didn't have to come here."

"I haven't the foggiest idea otherwise," Bristol says. "It seems as though it's the closest possibility, that we should try before driving further."

"Yeah, I'm not arguing that. I'm just confused, I guess And confused that I'm confused."

"We takin' a walk, then?" Dolly asks. She's apparently not worried that I'm confused, so okay. It's fine. I'm confused because I'm distracted and I'm distracted because I've got so much stuff happening in my systems to try and chase down the gamerunners, and see if they match with the agency, keep an eye on surrounding security systems so that we get maybe any kind of warning if somebody decides to move on us, the list goes on.

"I *did* want to see the outside sculptures," Bristol says confidingly. "And since the video says that we must walk through them…"

"Look, we got nothing but time," Dolly says, grinning at her and winking at me. "Right Bits?"

"Yeah we've only been doing this..." I check *that* timer. "39 hours."

"Oh is that all," Bristol says, a little faintly.

We go back out the way we came, before that guard comes to find us and kick us out, or we have to talk to any other security, and hang a right through the sculpture garden. I didn't expect to feel one way or another about this but I don't like it, actually. Nothing against the statues themselves, I don't think, but standing among statues instead of looking at them well-lit in an exhibition hall is something that makes my brain try to play the Uncanny Valley game. Are these people? Did that one just move? Are they about to move? A lot of them are on pedestals, and some are laying down.

One of them is a giant set of closed doors that the local map guide helpfully tells me is called The Gates of Hell before we have to walk through some vertical trees, and I can see that something about this is bothering Dolly too, maybe not the statues, but the walking through the suddenly kind of empty college campus, when not too long ago there were a lot of people. There are a lot of wooden benches here, scattered under trees and on the gravel or whatever this is, all vacant. Somebody left a bouquet of blue flowers in front of The Gates of Hell, at the feet of the statue labeled Eve, and Bristol stoops to examine them for a second, picking something up and tucking it in her pocket.

"Bristol, what—" She shakes her head, her tight smile telling me that she's caught my mood.

We pass between the straight trees or bushes or whatever they are, they remind me of pictures from the Roman countryside, and it's darker over here as we walk towards the road that we'll take to where the painting was set. Except it doesn't really quite exist as such anymore, that I can tell, but if there's a clue it can be taped to a light pole for all we know. Maybe as one of those advertisements with the little pull-off tabs; you can make those that are flat little USB drives, and not that most of us would just plug a random USB into an unsecured device, but if you were participating in the game you might.

It's a relief when Dolly asks, "Does it bother anybody else that we're walkin' down quarry road?"

"I thought you'd never mention it, darling."

"Bits?"

"Yeah but I don't see a problem yet. Which might be the problem." I sync up my scanner app with the local law enforcement networks. Their chatter is boring and minimal, nothing indicating that they're gearing up/have geared up for anything unusual or interagency.

"It's quiet, a little too quiet?"

"Yeah."

To our left is just hospital buildings, a whole hospital compound, and to our right is more museum or campus property, a cactus garden, the map says.

"Do we think they can hear us?" Bristol looks around without looking around, something we're all pretty good at by now.

I shrug, because it's always possible. "Maybe."

//We're gonna have to scatter, I think// Dolly says in our earbuds, using the subaudible system.

//Not too early// Bristol answers, and I nod.

//Bristol, power the game phone off. Do we all have our cloaking devices?// I ask. Mine's in one of my pockets, I don't know if Bristol's is in her purse or not. Who knows what Bristol has in her purse. I also assume Dolly's got one in a pocket.

//I do, yes.//

//Sure do. Drop a marker on a meetup, Bitsy.// I look at what's nearby on the map. A fine dining restaurant that all of us but Bristol would get kicked out of, and I light that up for her as possible scatter location. It would be predictable to the agency though, so who knows. A coffee shop. Further, more museums, all of them closed. A couple of hotels or motels. A lot of shopping centers, all of them closed for the night. Some residential neighborhoods. The mall might be good; there'll be overnight cleaning staff, maybe, but probably it'll be automated. Organizations like automating. And I can take care of entry.

//The amount of time we spend physically running...// Bristol says, trailing off with a sigh, taking out her active camouflage device, and that's when we hear the sudden approach of engines, pushed a little faster than we'd normally expect on this little back road, no sirens so it's not ambulances for the hospital. No headlights reflect off the street signs; they're running dark.

"Now," Dolly says, and we split, Dolly directly to the right across a short open expanse and into the trees, or I assume into the trees, because she disappears as she moves, the active camo doing its job. Bristol and I break left across the street, keying our devices, and I hear her taking stairs that hook up behind a bus shelter, me running straight into a little foyer ahead of closed hospital doors. This might be a mistake, I think, I'm good at doors but am I *this* good at doors, these don't have *handles*, but a narrow line of light is visible between them and I scrabble my fingers at the gap and pull one open, slip in, knock the wadded plastic out of the latch that kept it from closing. Maybe this is the door employees slip out of to smoke. Maybe this is the door family members use to come in after hours, I don't know, and I'm sorry I can't leave it the way I found it right now but it's better if it closes right now.

No visible cameras, and nobody in the hallway, and I jog up it as quietly as I can before turning down the first hallway that I see, and then the next. This is not the patient or visitors part of the hospital, this is definitely staff realm. I even pass somebody pushing a cart full of supplies and they pause like they hear me and so I pause so that they don't, and they walk on. I find a bathroom to go into and decloak, then wash my hands and walk out like I'm supposed to be there visiting or whatever. It's better to save the battery, for when I leave and cross all of those streets and parking lots.

I haven't spent a lot of time in hospitals, luckily, but there's so much interesting equipment networked here. I sign onto the public network just with the phone I've been using, and then backdoor into the broader connections, and I'm floored by all of the stuff that they have online. Lots of sensitive information systems, lots of sensitive medical equipment. The wrong person could do a lot of damage, even accidentally. Granted, *most* people won't even think to do what I've done, they just want to be on social media to talk to people while they're here, or they want to stream their shows, or whatever. But it was easy for me to get in and it was easy for me to plug in, and that's something I think about for later. The records systems probably have more layers of protection that I don't see because I'm not touching them, they must. Their security people have to know better, right?

But it's not my problem, I can't make it my problem right now. I stop at a water fountain to catch my breath and drink. I always need to drink more water. //Check check// Dolly says quietly into our earbuds, and it's about when I thought she'd check in, and check on us, but I'm so relieved all the same.

//Check// I say.

//Check// Bristol says, sounding out of breath still.

//Holding pattern?// Dolly asks.

//Yes, alright// Bristol says. She's gotten to the restaurant, I think, and I imagine she's in the ladies' room taking the five magical minutes she can use to look unruffled and put together.

//Understood// I say, and look for a waiting room.

Chapter Ten

We stay apart for a few hours, long enough for Bristol to have a light meal, and have several drinks paid for by men at the restaurant, and for me to watch our parking meter run down and our car get towed away to a nearby impound lot. I don't know what Dolly does; she's active, and she checks in periodically, but doesn't narrate or enlighten us. She doesn't like that I want to go to the mall first, but I want to be sure of the security systems letting us in, and I've got active camo too.

I leave the hospital maybe a little earlier than I say that I was going to, because there's only so comfortable I feel milling around a hospital in the middle of the night. If I could focus on just that, it'd be one thing, but I can't. I've kept an eye on the entrances, remotely, when I could, to make sure no agency sweeps came in looking. That I can tell, nobody out of place did, other than me. Maybe I saw some homeless people sneak in but, no I didn't. Absolutely not my business.

Once I'm out of sight from the hospital and am in an intersection of shadows, because of signs and trees and low buildings, I activate the camo. It's interesting, because I can't see myself either, and it's best not to think too much about that or it's easy to get really tripped up. I'm sure we all had some really funny private practice sessions, getting used to these. Or maybe it was part of Dolly's super soldier training, who knows. Well, I could know, I have her files. I only look at them when she asks me to, though, not just because I wonder about something.

It's possible I don't need it, but also I don't want to walk across a big huge parking lot alone in the middle of the night when people are actively after us without it. I wonder what made the agency jumpy, that they wanted to reel us in now. Or maybe they've been working on this since Bristol's wedding, or since Dolly had her little meeting with Will, and it took this long for the request to pass through committee and the plan to be planned. I probably should've keyed in sooner, like at the mechanical bull. Or when there was literally a bouquet of flowers for a clue.

Were the blue flowers at the sculpture garden meant as warning, or were they just a coincidence? I search blue roses while I walk, and the internet consensus seems to be that they're meant to signify mystery. I'm sure Bristol knows that, she mentioned flowers having meaning.

I get to the mall entrance, and of course the automatic doors don't open. I have a look for infrared sensors, motion detectors, all of that, and find the panel for the security keypad. A pretty standard, widely used model, and I hold down the two buttons that'll give me admin access and type 1234#, and the panel flashes green and I hear a click of the door releasing.

Slipping inside, I'm not really sure this mall is currently functioning. A cursory glance at the website had recently updated hours and tenants, but looking at it again, not all of the indoor stores are still functioning, and the most recently updated store only has outdoor access. Even better, for us. It's clean in here, no debris on the floor, no graffiti, but it smells dusty and empty. It's unbelievably quiet; the HVAC must not be on, I realize after a while that there isn't the ever-present, almost subaudible hum from that.

//It's clear// I say.

//I'll be arriving in a few moments// Bristol says in less than five minutes, according to my stopwatch. The silence from Dolly stretches out. She heard me, I know she had to hear me. She doesn't always answer right away, depending on positioning. This isn't outside of normal Dolly parameters.

The time keeps ticking up and I'm about to go looking for Dolly's electronic signature, which I'd held off on doing so that no local surveillance would notice extra packet traffic, when she says //Gonna be a little while longer, just sit tight. I'm okay.//

//Understood// I say, not understanding but isn't all of this a trust fall, and I go to the door to let Bristol in.

"What is she *doing*?" Bristol asks in an alarmed, loud whisper. Her eyes are taking in the abandoned setting as I trip the manual lock on the door again. She's changed her clothes, into her couture version of riot gear finally, though I don't know how she had all of it in her bag. It's a big bag, that's the only answer I need, I guess. One of those purses that's a big leather tote bag.

I shrug as we move away from the doors again. "I don't know. Dolly things."

"Very helpful, Bits darling." She sighs and then looks at me. "I'm so sorry that isn't fair. None of us are Dolly's keeper. I just worry that she's doing something dangerous, to keep the two of us safe."

"I do too. But we have to trust that she isn't. I don't think we're to that point right now." The only time, before, that we had been to that point, Bristol is the one who led away the hunters while Dolly and I, incapacitated in various ways, got to help and then safety. We're canny quarry, if nothing else. Plus, if you ask any outsider, they would say that they absolutely would not believe that Bristol would do such a thing.

We wait in what had once been a hallway for vending machines that led to public restrooms, near the doors we'd come in but not visible from them. There's holes in the wall for water fountains, but they're gone now, and their pipes. Uninstalled, or stolen for scrap. Which means the bathroom fixtures are probably also all gone. I look at the vending machines, dark-faced but their glass intact. Canned coffee and tea and energy drinks, bottled water, snacks assortment. Normally, because we live in a society, I wouldn't have the opportunity to just walk up to one of these things and use the vending machine key that I have, in a bundle of universally available keys if you know the right stores to buy from, but this is absolutely that opportunity and I need to distract myself for a few minutes, and I'm getting really tired actually and if there's still canned coffee or energy drinks in one of these, it might still be good. Or might not be poison, anyway. How 'bad' can coffee actually go? I'm not really sure.

"Bits, darling, what are you doing?" Bristol asks when I swing the first machine open.

"I know you just had dinner, but I could use a snack," I say. The first one's empty, well, beverages-empty but full of spiderwebs, and I shut it again. The second one has cans, dusty but brightly colored, and I'm reaching for one when Dolly comes in on the earbuds.

//Okay, I'm inbound, come let me in.//

"Thank goodness," Bristol says. She looks at her phone. "Oh, Ant has been texting me. I think that perhaps I shouldn't answer?"

"What's he saying?"

"The usual are you okay sorts of things. He does seem quite worried."

"You can tell him you're okay, if you want," I say. "You're using the app that—"

She smiles; Bristol's frivolous socialite façade makes it easy to forget that she's actually always as in control of herself and situation as she can be. "The secure one you make us all use to run our messages through, that scrambles our location in the occasion somebody attempts to trace it? Mais oui."

"Good then. Yeah, it's fine. It'll probably keep him from doing something stupid." We go to meet Dolly.

"Surely we'll stop somewhere to sleep now?"

"Probably, but it also should be like, a safehouse and not just any old hotel. Given our alert level."

"Oh yes, of course," she murmurs, only the slightest layer of veneer over her disappointment.

Bristol hangs back and I unlock the door for Dolly, who has Bristol's overnight bag, and her duffel, and mine. "I went and got our stuff from the car," she says, as I'm locking the door again.

"You're such a sweetheart," Bristol says, at the same time I'm saying, "Dolly, what?"

She grins, looking between the two of us. "Well they just had local law enforcement tow the car, and nobody looked at it right away. I don't know if they have agents coming in later or tomorrow or what. So I trailed them to the impound lot and then hopped the fence. I know how attached Bristol is to her shoes, I didn't want to owe her another pair."

"Darling, you know that wasn't actually your fault, and I've more than forgiven you by now."

"Sure, yeah, fool me once..." Dolly says, still grinning. "There isn't much creepier'n an abandoned mall, huh?"

"Cemeteries, I would think," Bristol says after a slight pause.

"Nah, they're not empty."

I laugh, surprised. "Jesus, Dolly."

"Well they're not!" I shake my head and sigh, and it turns into a yawn. "Okay, what's the plan? We crashing here tonight?"

"Heavens no," Bristol says, even more horrified than when I opened the vending machines. "Absolutely not, I would rather turn myself in."

"Aw, you don't mean that, Bristles," Dolly says, but she does look a little repentant. "Anyways, getting our next ride'll be easy enough, there are plenty of targets. We probably can't rent anything on account of the surveillance dragnet and all."

"And then where will we *go*?" Bristol asks.

"Well I assume back to Vegas to kick some nerd ass, but I'm open to suggestions."

"A hotel first, since Bristol doesn't want to sleep under a bridge or whatever, but maybe near the airport? Or further? And then tomorrow we'll have Bristol call that number Ant so nicely gave her, and I'll trace his location and devices and then we'll track him down and get some answers." It's already tomorrow, but tomorrow is after you get up.

"Couldn't you find him anyway without..." Dolly trails off.

"Yeah, but I want him to lie to her one more time, knowing what we know." I don't like catching people in crossfire.

"Atta girl."

"An airport hotel is the best idea, I'd say" Bristol says. "So many comings and goings, we'll be all the more unobtrusive."

"You've never wanted that in your life," I say, before Dolly has the chance, and Bristol gives a little laugh.

"We all know each other so well, don't we?"

We walk towards the exit at the other end of the mall; we'd already had so much activity at the doors I cracked, I'd rather circumvent security again than rely on that working out one last time. "Still think it's creepy," Dolly grumbles.

"But there's so much space!" Bristol says brightly. "You could turn cartwheels or rollerskate or..."

"Now Bristles, I didn't know you knew how to turn a cartwheel."

"Doesn't everybody?" She turns to me. "Bits, you can do a cartwheel, right?"

"Yeah," I say. It's been a while, but is that a thing you forget? I stop and put my bags down, look at the floor to make sure that I'm not about to put my hands in broken glass, and run the motion through my head, raising my hands and then bending to the floor before I could overthink it. Kind of sloppy, but I do it. Bristol claps, delighted, and Dolly laughs.

"Well okay, everybody can do a cartwheel. Supposedly." She does one too, and then when she lands does a backflip. "Sorry, gotta show off sometimes right? You understand, Bristles."

"Of course, darling," Bristol says, laughing and clapping her hands again. She hands me her bag."I'm afraid I am more at

Bits's skill level." It isn't often that I think Bristol isn't telling us the truth; this might be the first time. Her cartwheel doesn't seem at all rusty, it's comfortable, like she's done them for her whole life or maybe practiced a lot. Maybe it's just that Bristol doesn't like doing anything unless it seems like she's good at it.

Dolly claps too, and I think it's maybe one of the first times all three of us have stood around laughing together like a group of friends doing friend things. We work really well together, and have for a couple of years now, but friendship is a thing that can be both weirdly narrow and really encompassing all at the same time, and we just don't always connect like that. Maybe it's mostly Bristol that keeps everybody at an arm's length on purpose; I've thought Dolly and I were actually friends versus colleagues for longer. But did that mean we didn't try harder, with Bristol? Or were we just letting her come around on her own terms? Well, if it bothered her, we'd know.

We all brush off our hands because even though the floor isn't fuzzy with dust, there is some, and Bristol offers around hand sanitizer. I wonder again about the cleanliness in here; I really think that it's probably robot vacuums or whatever but still haven't seen any stations for them. They could just be down a janitorial hallway, an offshoot like the vending hallway Bristol and I were in for that little while.

I yawn hard and long enough that my eyes water before I get to work on this door. I'm tired enough that it takes a little more time, disengaging the security, manually clicking the lock, but I get there without tripping any other systems, defensive or cleaning or anything else, and we're back out into the night, and after I kind of do a general sweep of network chatters and police type vehicles, we risk a rideshare that's driving by with its lights hopefully on.

"You girls are out late," the driver says, eyeing us in her rear view mirror. "It's good you're all buddied up like that."

"Of course we always practice safety in numbers," Bristol says. She's sitting in the front seat, looking at her phone.

"That's smart. Wish I could do that driving, but I can't."

"You could get a robot dog," Dolly says, gives me a look of wide-eyed innocence when I elbow her. "What? You can charge them at charge stations and some of them are *specifically* for security."

"Too expensive," the driver says. "I just have a gun instead."

Dolly laughs. "Yeah, that'll do you."

They chatter about guns the rest of the way to the hotel, Dolly leaning between the front seats, and I reserve a room for us at the hotel, running our payment through and getting three days. We won't stay the whole time but that gives us a landing pad that we can use while we're here, and then as a decoy if we need to. It's an automated hotel, so no staff to contend with other that the maintenance staff who periodically come around, but they won't be there when we are, and they won't care about who we are.

I also check my messages, check on the other team's map location. New Mexico. It really is two different games, a real one, or real-adjacent anyway, and a trap one. I really did want that IBM chip, I think ruefully, but that's what they were counting on. I'll just have to find a tech dump or something, comb through satellite photos for likely candidates. The prizes were just too fine-tuned for our interests. Well, they took a gamble on Dolly caring about the motorcycle I guess. Or Bristol.

Wouldn't that be funny, if it turned out that she was just really into 20th century anime? Nobody would expect that. But if it was necessary, with some study, she could make pretty much anybody believe it.

I organize my files of the teams that aren't real teams, and flag the names that I thought I recognized. Then I run a search on the names that I don't recognize, across as many platforms as my crawlers can reasonably reach in a short time, and one by one, a lot of them come up dry. Some are real, and I run location traces on all of them. Most of us, 'hackers' us, run layers of location foiling, VPNs and redirects and all of that, but I just want approximate hits, I neither want nor expect genuine and accurate real time home addresses. I just want to confirm that they aren't actually clumped in teams in the Western half of the United States.

While that's running, we get to the hotel, and get our stuff out of the car. Our room is on the third floor, windows overlooking the road. Once we're inside, I take Dolly's phone for a minute and sign it onto the hotel wireless; I want to see how many people are locally active, and that's the simplest way without adding another thing to my systems, which can handle it, but I've got so many windows open, I don't want to shuffle them around again. It's a weekday, so our potential neighbors are pretty sparse. Only four other rooms are occupied, and there are two on the first floor, one on the second, and one on the fourth, good.

We walk up the outer ramp to our floor, and I copy those device markers and hand Dolly back her phone. "What're we looking at?" she asks.

"Only a few other people here, and we're alone on this floor." It's possible there are people here who aren't online, but almost everybody has at least one device that hops onto available wireless whether you want it to or not. I check my scanner app. "Nothing on the scanners."

"Just means they didn't involve the locals. Plus, the car was just a normal expired meter tow, not special fancy impound."

"Do you mind if I take a bath, darlings?" Bristol asks.

"No, go for it," I say. The room is long, railroad car style, with a little entry hall that's got a closet space, then a room with a big tv and two double beds, and then the other bedroom, with a king sized bed and huge windows that Bristol walks briskly to and pulls the shades on.

"I'm starving," Dolly says. "Anybody want anything? Gonna see what's on the hoof in the vending machines. Maybe at that 7-Eleven we passed on the way in."

"I'm just going to check on some stuff and I'm passing out," I say.

"Okay, but if it's dawn and you're still awake, I'm gonna take your toys away and put them in a tinfoil box."

"You won't know if I'm still awake," I say, laughing.

"That's what you think." She makes the 'eyes on you' gesture, then takes the keycard from me and goes out again.

I kick my boots off and crawl across one of the double beds. "7-Eleven," Bristol says with a sigh, as she closes the bathroom door.

"She likes 7-Eleven."

"Trust me, I am well aware."

Chapter Eleven

I'm still awake when Dolly comes back, but I'm finishing up with the fake team data and not really paying attention until I hear Bristol laughing. I've got a long list of people that don't seem to exist other than sockpuppet accounts with stock image avatars, and a short list of people who very much do exist and who are flung across the globe and country and don't seem to be in this area of operation. Though that also gives me a list of people to check agency files on next time I slip into their systems, and it's a list of people that need some kind of a warning.

I check the time; I definitely dozed for some of the time she was gone. I think. It's hard to tell sometimes. I push my headset up and blink at them. I can still see steam on the bathroom mirror, so I guess it hasn't been so long. Bristol is in one of the plush hotel robes, but her hair is dry. Already, or still?

"They had pairings on the shelf tags!" Dolly's saying in protest, but also laughing. "Is that wrong?"

"No, darling, I very much appreciate the thought."

"Then what's the problem? I brought choices. Pinot and grapes, rosé and watermelon. I assumed the fruit was like, the least adulterated thing I could get there, so you might eat it. Because I could've gotten the single-serve carton of chardonnay and their shrimp skewers."

"Thank you for not purchasing shrimp skewers for me at 7-Eleven," Bristol says in a careful, measured voice. "Sorry, Bits, did we wake you?"

"No," I say. "But it's not late enough that Dolly's going to take my stuff away. Early enough."

"It's gettin' there," Dolly says with her mouth full, shaking her fist.

"Then why are you making so much noise?" I ask, blinking at her. That surprises her, and she suddenly ceases all movement, trying to see if I'm joking or not, and I crack a smile as I put my headset on the bedside table.

Bristol cracks open one of the canned wines and sniffs it hesitantly. "Just a nightcap," she says, as though we're watching her judgmentally.

"Is it to m'lady's taste?" Dolly asks, and then shudders. "Hah, forget I said it like that."

"Yes, let's."

"Bitsy, I got you canned cold brew for when we get up, not now."

"Thank you," I say. It's funny, how much she's scolding me. She's the one who woke us up at 5:30 a.m. to get on the road. Bristol absolutely would not have picked that time. I wouldn't have picked that time.

They go into the room with the king sized bed to eat and bicker, and I get changed, wash up in the bathroom, then actually lay down to sleep, not even putting my headset back on. We hit all the activity high notes today, driving in the car for hours, and then physically running, interspersed with a lot of VR and other hacking type activities. I fall asleep before 5:30 a.m. at least, so I didn't stay up for a full twenty four hours. I've done it before, and I'm sure I'll do it again, just not today. Before I drop off, I reach out for the room remote and paw the controls until the door chimes that it's been set to Do Not Disturb, and then I fall asleep before I'm able to put the remote back on the bedside table.

I come partway awake once, when I hear my phone vibrate with a notification, but Dolly and Bristol are clearly sleeping still, no noise from either of them, and I just roll over and figure the notifications can wait. We don't do anything until we're all rested, at this point, unless something dire is happening, and if something dire is happening, my phone will buzz more than once. More will happen than my phone buzzing.

I *really* sleep after that, waking up when Dolly stumbles to the bathroom and turns the shower on. I hope it isn't 5:30 again; I roll onto my back and stretch, check my HUD. No, almost noon. It's a miracle.

She put one of the cans of coffee next to my phone and headset as she passed by; my fingers graze it when I reach for the phone, and come away cold. I've got a bunch of notifications, a lot of them in the spam filter, which I always check because sometimes it's interesting or at least funny. Rarely useful, though. The buzz right as I was falling asleep was the flag that I have on Will's biometrics. He can change devices, but with his clearances, he can't change his fingerprints and retinas, they're in the system. What system? All of them. They're not always labeled the same way of course but the data is the data.

He didn't land in the airport we're sleeping next to; nope, he's in Las Vegas, which is still where the gamerunners are. I assume we'll fly there, I don't think Bristol is eager to get back in the car for another eight hours. Should we run away from Will instead of towards? Yeah probably. But they also won't expect this. And probably don't expect that we know what's going on. They can't not underestimate us, apparently, and I wonder why that is. We sat in a room with Will and his supervisor and we all signed contracts and then Marquis is the only one who kept to it. And yet the agency is still just shocked, shocked at the state of affairs regarding us. Do they just think Will is particularly bad at this? Do they think that, because they got the most important diamonds and data back, we aren't worth pursuit? It's true that while we stole those diamonds on purpose, we didn't steal the top clearance intel on purpose. It's also been true that Will, at least, is still after us, but hasn't been good enough on his own.

I sit up and grab the coffee, pop the tab before I notice that it says to shake. Typical. I take a sip off the top, and then kind of swirl the can in my hand like it's a glass of brandy. I can't tell the difference between my next sip and my first one. Shaking the can might be a scam, or at least with this brand.

Bristol sighs and rolls over when Dolly starts whistling in the shower. "Good morning," I say, and she kind of hums. "Do you want one of my canned coffees that Dolly got?"

"Thank you, darling, but no."

"You won't want anything at the airport."

"No, but if we fly first class, what they have will be suitable."

"If we don't?" Should I have reserved flights already, or did one of them do that? We were so tired.

"We are in the business of solving problems, aren't we?" She stands up and stretches luxuriantly, then twitches apart the curtains to look outside. "Oh, I'd forgotten the airport was our view."

"Sunrise over the tarmac," I say, and we laugh.

The shower cuts off and I drink my coffee and scroll through all of my notifications and updates. The other team is doing pretty well; they won't beat last year's winner on time, I think they've got more than one clue left. Maybe they don't, who knows. Two games diverged in the desert, and we took the ones planned by a government agency, question mark. In a not-really way, our time is much better than last year's team; we already figured out that the game is rigged.

I don't realize they're talking to me until Dolly hits me with balled-up foil. "What?"

"I was askin' if you got us flights already or if we need to do that."

"I wondered the same thing," I say.

"For heaven's sake," Bristol says, but she's smiling.

"Okay, so we need tickets to Vegas so we can kick some nerd ass. Unless we want to drive to Vegas?"

"No, thank you," Bristol says at the same time I say, "Probably not."

I check into flights, and Dolly makes coffee with the room's coffee maker and complimentary bag of grounds, reading the package with surprising concentration. "So I'm skeptical that people are growing fair trade coffee in North Dakota, that's weird, right?"

"I mean, it's probably in green houses?"

"In quantity to be robot hotel supply coffee?"

I shrug. "Maybe it's a selling point, it's this hotel exclusive or something."

"Or it's a lie."

"Just the fictions of marketing, darling," Bristol says, breezing through to the bathroom with her makeup bag. "First class, if it's available?"

"If it's available," I say, clicking through. We can check in at 1:30, which is soon but not too soon I don't think, be wheels up at 2:15 and in Las Vegas by 4:15.

"Nice to have the leg room, even on a short flight."

"Really short flight," I say, organizing my records of the IDs we're using on this trip, running the reservations and then doing the pre-flight check in once the notifications hit my inbox. I do the mental math quick to make sure I'm not forgetting, but we won't have to check any bags. "Dolly do you need firearms clearance?"

"Nah, I'm good."

I look at her. "You haven't had a gun this whole time?"

She grins, and the brew cycle gurgles to a finish behind her. "I didn't say that."

"But—"

"I can make a drop and then pick up somethin' new on the other side, I do it all the time." She pours a mug of the coffee and sniffs it before she takes a sip. It smells like pretty normal coffee from here. "Tastes like coffee," she says with a shrug.

"It smells over roasted," Bristol says from the bathroom.

"Lotta people like that. Or, they emperor's-new-clothesed themselves into thinking they like it."

"There's probably a less awkward way to say that," I say.

"Yeah, prob'ly." She takes another sip. "Wanna try?"

"Sure." It tastes okay, I guess; not burnt. I forget that Dolly drinks her coffee black, even though I just watched her make it. "Oh hey."

"Hey yourself," she says, taking the cup back. "What's up?"

"Will is also in Las Vegas."

"Since when?" Dolly asks, and Bristol comes to the bathroom door, holding her uncapped mascara.

"Late last night slash early this morning. After we went to bed. Well, after I went to bed, I don't technically know when you did."

"Wonder why," Dolly says.

"It's probably easiest for Will to work with the gamerunners in person at this portion of the operation," Bristol says thoughtfully. "And he doesn't want Bits to be privy to their conversations, should she be listening to them electronically."

"Will does have a healthy respect for Bitsy's prowess, that is true."

"And he thinks you're a cold-blooded killer without a shred of humanity."

"I mean, I am," she says, offering Bristol the coffee cup. Bristol shakes her head and goes back to the mirror. "He ain't the first one I've had that effect on."

"I'm sure," Bristol says.

"Anyway, you like it," I say, tossing my coffee can in the wastebasket.

"Of course I do, he isn't any use to me in the traditional way. Too goddamn wholesome."

"Right." She gets the other canned coffee out of the little hotel fridge and I nod when she waggles it at me. "So what's the actual plan for Vegas?"

"What, we need more of a plan than kicking nerd ass?"

"With Will present, we do," Bristol points out.

"I can kick his ass too," Dolly says cheerfully.

"Okay, but I mean, are we gonna steal the stuff that was supposed to be the prizes?"

"Yeah we could do that," Dolly says. "If it's real."

"They've still got one live team playing a game, something is real."

"There's something so sad about that," Bristol says, zipping up her makeup bag and coming out again. "They're doing the work and losing sleep, thinking that they're in a viable competition but they're only competing against the illusion of other teams."

"They know that we're in it," I say. "But not that there's like. Game/real game dynamics."

"Aww, poor buddies," Dolly says. "We can kick 'em some cash if you want, Bristles."

"I didn't say—"

"You didn't, but you also feel bad for people so rarely, we gotta reinforce that right?"

"Honestly, Dolly darling, I—"

"And I'm the one Will thinks is cold blooded," Dolly says, winking at me, but I'm chugging the second can of coffee to avoid having to say anything. I didn't shake this one either. Bristol, smiling fixedly, finishes packing her things.

"We all have our roles," she says after almost exactly a minute. Fifty five seconds.

"True, we do. So where are we going and what're we doing?"

I start digging in my kit; I should've been thinking about this and slept instead, but also in my defense, some of last night was spent sprinting and that's not a normal part of things. "Before we leave the hotel, we're going to have Bristol call the personal number she was given, using the game burner phone, which we'll leave here and go catch our flight. I'm making a clone now, though, so we don't lose access to that number and connection. She'll say that since we're unable to continue the game, we'll have to bow out, and thank them for the good time. Implying that we're skipping town, skipping the country, whatever. We'll see what they say from there. We know Bristol's good at improvising."

"Thank you, darling."

"We packed, then?" Dolly asks, then surveys the room, which other than the unmade beds looks like we just got here. "Okay."

I hand Bristol the phone, and she dials the number into it from hers. She leaves her earbud in, so Dolly and I can hear the whole conversation. Ant answers on the third ring. "Hey, what's up?"

"Good morning, darling, I'm afraid I have some bad news."

"What is it? Are you okay?" Dolly raises her eyebrows at me; he does sound genuinely concerned, I'll give him that. Some of that probably has to do with our team geotag just being in one place in the hours since the car was towed. Maybe he doesn't know, he's not the partner who's in on it with the agency. But he has to be, they can't possibly not all know that most of the teams are fake.

"It would seem that we are unable to complete the game, as things stand, so we will have to regretfully bow out. It is *such* a shame, this was great fun."

"Unable to complete...what happened out there?" There's muffled talking somewhere near him. Other gamerunners, Will, whoever Will brought with him expecting us to make contact. It might be Null again, that would be awkward. Theo-retically.

"We just ran into a teensy snag and then didn't get the next clue and now we need to leave town without having done so, much to our deepest regrets. We thought we were doing so well and now disaster!"

"Yes, you were the leading team, yeah that's a shame. Are you...okay? Do you need one of us to come get you? From somewhere?" He still sounds pretty genuine, and I wonder if this got set up in part as a test case for Will, so he could see somebody else just helpless in Bristol's hands and maybe not feel so bad about being as smitten as he is. Seems possible.

"No, no, there's no need for that. We're fine, we're probably even safe. We're simply between a rock and a hard place."

There's rustling on the other end of the line, and some short, hushed argument, and then a new voice comes on the line.

"Did something really happen, or can you just not figure it out? You'd rather lose the whole game than ask for a hint?"

"Now that isn't very pleasant, is it?" Bristol says mildly, rolling her eyes.

Dolly mouths *Good nerd, bad nerd* and we all smile.

"It's unusual for an all-female team to try something like this."

"You'd be amazed at how often we run into comments like that, darling, it really isn't as original as you must have assumed. We needn't try to twist this into a women's issue, when re-ally, you're trying to obfuscate the actual problem with your little game." She looks at me and Dolly, questioning. I check the timer and then hold up my thumb and forefinger: close to when she should hang up and we should leave. She nods.

It was the right thing to send this guy off, though. "Our *little* game? You mean our very successful game with big prizes that you volunteered for, if you're forgetting."

Bristol smiles, as though he can see her, and then says softly, indulgently, "Oh, darling. We know there are only two teams." She hangs up on his startled exclamation and drops the phone on the bed, as it immediately starts ringing.

"He had to know we knew, right?" Dolly asks, looking at the bed.

"It's hard to say," Bristol says. "But he's certainly upset about it, either way. Plus that female team nonsense. These men need better peers."

"He was probably trolling on purpose." I pick up my bags.

"In my experience, people who like trolling never got the assbeatings they deserved."

"Maybe not," I say. "But there's a first time for everything."

We go out and get a rideshare to the airport, visible from our hotel but of course not walkable. I check out of the hotel as we go, then check our pre-check for the flight and that's all smooth sailing. Security is even less of a pain than it could be about our equipment, the reinforcements in our clothes that are clearly visible on their scans, my computer stuff. I think sending Dolly through first, and the Bristol, is the right plan. That way they see Dolly's cybernetic arm and smell the money and class coming off of Bristol, and by the time they get to me, they have a plausible narrative that they told themselves.

Chapter Twelve

We reserve a hotel for a few days and stow our luggage, and Bristol and I go to a diner off the strip and get coffee (me) and sparkling water (her) while we wait for Dolly to take care of some business, as she said. I get nachos for the sake of having something to pick at while I chase the connections that the gamerunners have locally, to see how many people it's likely that we have to worry about when we go confront them. It doesn't seem like they expect us to be here. I could be wrong, but it doesn't seem like it.

The waitress does entice Bristol into some sort of pastry by the time Dolly arrives; apparently this place has a French-trained pastry chef for some reason. I guess I shouldn't say for some reason, people end up all kinds of places for all kinds of reasons. Maybe they're from here and went to France to train and bring it back right here. I'm not going to go interview them for a profile.

"Sorry that took so long," Dolly says. She doesn't seem out of breath or particularly ruffled. It didn't really even take all that long.

"It's no matter, darling, it just means we'll be able to see the sunset from the high rise hotel that they're in."

Dolly laughs. "Yeah you're right, it'll be a real romantic backdrop to the proceedings." She looks at the table, looks at us. "So are we ready?"

"I guess."

"Of course."

We go outside and I check one last time where the gamerunners are, crosschecking them with nearby devices. Then I do the same for Will. Still the same place. There seems to be just the three of them in the room, and while I don't know if that's really true, I just have to trust that we can handle that many or more. Mostly Dolly, but...

We walk up the street, cut a block over, and then walk through a hotel lobby to the elevator. "Okay, once we get up there, let's all use our camo so that we can do the 'knock on the door but the hallway looks empty when somebody looks out the keyhole' thing, I've always wanted to do that."

"Jesus Christ, Dolly," I say, but I can't help laughing. "Sure, yeah, we can do that. Right Bristol?"

"It will be very cinematic," she says thoughtfully.

"We watch different movies," Dolly points out, and then I shush them both, because we're two floors away and I don't want anybody to hear us talking. I text them the room number.

We activate our camo before the elevator opens; the hallway is empty, which is good. We try to avoid collateral damage. We go down the hallway to the door, and the floor is pretty quiet, either by happy accident or by agency/gamerunner design, it's hard to guess and I don't want to take the time to investigate right now. I stop to the side of the door, and assume Bristol does the same. Dolly knocks, shave and a haircut, and we wait.

There's a pause; I hadn't been aware of people talking in the room until they stopped. I watch the peephole, and a shadow passes over it when somebody looks through. Another pause, and Ant mutters, "That's weird, there's nobody there." He's got the bolt off and the knob turned when Will says

"No, wait!" but then the door flies open, coupled with un-mistakable sound of a boot sole flat on wood. Ant stumbles back a few feet and then falls with a grunt, and I catch the waft of Bristol's perfume as she moves into the room and I go in too, closing the door behind us and bolting it again.

The guy on the floor gets invisibly dragged into the sitting room of the suite, like a horror movie, and the other gamerun-ner is just frozen in place, either through surprise or fear or Bristol tased him, and Will has his arm back for his holster but he's frozen too, his head tilted back just a little, and I realize no, that's where Bristol is, so I go to the other gamerunner and take the phone out of his loose fingers.

//On the three-count// I text on our network, and then we drop the active camo.

Dolly has her boot on Ant's chest on the floor and her arm straight out with her gun pointed at the face of the other one, and yeah, Bristol is standing next to Will's gun arm, with her hair down and one of her slim hairpin knives just against where his jaw meets his neck.

"Do we have to explain anything, or do you fellas under-stand how this is gonna go?" Dolly asks, grinning. Bristol un-holsters Will's gun with her free hand and tosses it to Dolly. The way the other three flinch as she catches it is audible.

"What do you want?" The standing gamerunner asks. Trace, that's his name. He's the main face for the whole thing.

"An explanation, so that we know if our guesses got close, and the prizes would be nice. This is a version of winnin' the game, ain't it?"

"Uh, sure, yes, it is."

"This is almost disappointing," Dolly says to me in a confidential tone, but not really any quieter. "Too easy. What else do you have planned, Will? Is a helicopter gonna pull up and hover out that window?"

He clears his throat. "No helicopter."

"Good." She glances down at Ant on the floor. "You gonna behave if I let you park on the couch?"

"Yes," he says, immediately.

"You?" she asks the other one and he nods. From the look on his face, he's never looked down the barrel of a gun before. So few of us have, honestly, before our association with Dolly. "Okay, I'm gonna take three steps this way and let you two be honest and go straight to the couch. Got it?" They both nod. "Good." She takes three steps back away from them, one gun pointed at each, and I back off too, away to the side where there's a table full of takeout bags, so I'm out of her muzzle sweep.

"Get Ant's phone too. And Will's," I say. Dolly gestures with her gun, and Ant reaches slowly for his phone, tosses it towards me. It thumps onto the plush carpet and I go pick it up. Will rolls his eyes to Bristol, who nods.

"Go on, darling, give Bits your phone," she says, just as comfortably and easily as if we were sharing around pictures at an event. He gets it out slowly, and I wonder what he's thinking. How to disarm Bristol, maybe. If he can do it and get to Dolly without being shot. What I'd do in the meantime. He hands me his phone. "He can sit on the couch with the others, can't he, Dolly?"

"Hmm, I dunno."

I go sit at the table with their phones and the one I've been using. "If he has a panic button, he already hit it when we came through the door. It's probably fine." I don't think he has a panic button, I think this is his project and he's here solo. Just like when he was chasing the story of Bristol's wedding. He was absolutely certain it was her, and desperate to have backup, but the timing just didn't work out for him and muddied the waters enough once we left that the system files he has on us still say it's a dubious situation. I was even able to delete evidence of the original wedding license, so just the one with Bristol's friend is the only one that exists. I'd assume this means Will's learned his lesson about getting screenshots, but maybe not.

I set the gamerunners phones with a dongle that I have to crack their passcodes, and when I go to unlock Will's phone, it wants a fingerprint. I blink at it, and look over at him; he's watching me at the moment, which is a surprise. He always only has eyes for Bristol, which is I guess part of what the problem has been. I take the time to smile at him, because yeah, I can get around it, but then I get up and bring the phone over to him. He doesn't need to know that I can spoof his fingerprints.

"Unlock it, please," I say. He reaches out to take it and I shake my head. "Try again." His jaw tightens, but he nods and just presses his finger to the place. I watch the phone, and its connections, but no alarm is triggered, no timer that he has to do a puzzle for or anything. "Thanks." He just frowns.

"So are there prizes, or were you just gonna ghost on the other team?" Dolly asks. The game runners look at each other uncomfortably, and look at Will.

"The other team was going to be informed that they won second place and be given a smaller monetary award," Will says after a moment of clear deliberation. He doesn't have an earbud in, but that's earbud behavior. Maybe he was hoping to think of something else in that gap.

"Easy enough to do mockups of the motorcycle and stuff for online viewin," Dolly says in a drawl, maybe to make Bristol frown, which she does. She's sitting on the arm of the vacant couch, putting her hair back up.

"Honestly, Dolly."

I go back to the table and copy the data off Will's phone. There isn't any point in ghosting it, it'll be cut off as soon as we leave here. Unless they assume I've ghosted it and leave the connection open as a trap or data point, but it's so obvious. Much like the game. Oh well, maybe we can do a real one a different year, that's way lower profile. Or, like Dolly auditioning for American Gladiators, that just isn't fair. I sigh.

"Is everything all right, Bits darling?"

"Yeah, unrelated," I say. They've been talking, I should pay attention. I try to run it back in my head, and yeah, it's what we expected. The gamerunners got caught red handed at something, and Will offered them this deal. "Give them the deal anyway, it's not their fault we knew."

"How *did* you know?" Trace bursts out. "Everything was compartmentalized."

"It was too easy," I say, blinking. "In some ways, the first and second clues were the only normal ones."

"You didn't get the clue at Stanford," Trace says.

"'Cause we were runnin' from Will's people, have some sense," Dolly says.

"Anyway, we were on our way to it, and I'm certain that right now, taunting us is not something you'll want to pursue." Bristol uses her phone to check her hair, then slips it into a pocket. "Now then, what shall we do with you boys?"

The gamerunners hadn't considered this, and Ant goes pale while Trace goes red. Will had considered this, but has to date been unable to predict our behavior, so why would now be any different?

In the pause, I say "I'm sending out a message to the other team's phone, that we won at 58.25 hours, but that second prize is still within their reach."

"Givin' them the money, Bitsy?" Dolly asks.

"They didn't know they'd be involved in this kind of stuff."

"Fair enough." I look at Bristol, who also nods.

"I agree, it's what's best."

Trace's phone is the one with the prize wallet, and I set up the contingency. When the other team finishes, it'll send their registered credentials the prize. "Done."

Ant says, faintly, "We're sorry about this, if that helps."

"Gotta save your own skin sometimes," Dolly says. "You about ready, Bits?"

"Almost." I give Will's files a quick scroll; pre-game, he's got a file of reported sightings of us, and I look at those one by one. We can't be impeccable with our security at all times, I can admit that, but only two of them are actually us. One is Bristol, in London, and the other one is Dolly in Mexico City. The other ten aren't, though, and Will's notes for each sighting are equally even handed, he talked himself out of being convinced on each one, but also saved them as the best ones, in case he was wrong.

While he's still got a connection to the agency, I put on my VR headset and follow it back. For a while now, a few years, I've been beating my head against how many staff the agency actually has, what they're a branch of, what their funding is like. They're smart, and I am only myself, so I'm slowly getting the picture but things are at all times changing. Will's clearance is pretty good, and I look at his profile's immediate connections. A few coworkers, Null included; even from looking at a bargain basement mocked up headset a couple years ago, I still recognize her style. The supervisor, of course. Their casework is varied; international thieves and hackers like us, some muscle, though Butler doesn't seem to be on their list or at least not this node's list. Nicolai is, but that's to be more than expected; I think he's on multiple agency lists around the world. A couple of Bristol's other friends are in a small watchlist, Marquis and some baroness and an art dealer. I copy all that to look at later, in case warnings are in order. Nearly everybody's on some kind of watchlist, anyway, you get there by breathing.

"Look, you don't benefit from hurting any of us," Will says.

"Unfortunately, darling, we would," Bristol says, and the look he gives her is more surprised than it should be. "I do think that removing you would remove our main pursuers." Dolly seems surprised too, tilting her head in Bristol's direction just a little bit, when she hadn't been before. The room is very still, the sunset now blasting it with orange light, throwing our shadows against the back wall.

"Is that what we wanna do?" Dolly asks the room.

"I don't know," I say. Okay, so I'm surprised too.

"You know that if you kill me, the agency will look for you based on that alone," Will says in a very composed voice.

"That is true," Bristol agrees, getting up off the couch and stalking over to stand next to Dolly. "And without your relentless focus, they'll have even less of a chance of finding us."

The gamerunners aren't made for this kind of movie bullshit, and their composure is cracking. "We didn't want anybody to get hurt," Ant says unsteadily. "That goes for him too, can't we all just walk away from this?"

"Surprise support, Will, ain't that nice?" Dolly asks. "They wouldn't be in this mess without you."

"I think it's probably shoot them all or let them all go," I say, stuffing phones in my pockets and wiping things down. "And we should do it soon."

"All or nothin', interesting Bitsy. Bristol?"

"This is a gambling town," she says slowly. She looks from Will over to me, and I'm not sure I quite understand the question in her face, but I think that I do, and I nod. "The choice is yours, Will. Come with us, and everybody walks away. Decline, and only we three walk away."

"I don't understand how—"

"Clock's ticking, Will Scarlet," Dolly says, thumbing back the hammer on the gun in her right hand. She's told me that you absolutely don't in general need to do that with guns anymore, but that it's one of those movie things that always produces an effect, like racking a shotgun, even though you'll lose a round.

He looks back at Dolly and I wonder what he's thinking. Then he swallows with an audible click and says, "I'll come with you." If the gamerunners weren't absolutely petrified in place, they would fall over with relief.

Bristol claps her hands once, and everybody on the couch jumps. Dolly smirks but doesn't laugh. "Excellent, darling." She looks around the room. "Do you have any luggage you need to collect?"

"The rolling suitcase there," he says, gesturing with his chin.

"Well get it, let's go," Dolly says. Will stands up, hesitantly, and walks to his suitcase in a daze, grabs the handle so it telescopes. "Gentlemen," she says nodding at the gamerunners. "It was fun while it lasted. Don't call the cops, if you know what's good for you." They nod in unison, like puppets.

I walk out ahead and call the elevator. I don't know if Dolly has a car lined up already, or if that's something we still need to do. We all stand in the elevator and watch the numbers go down. I don't know where Dolly disappeared Will's gun to, but it isn't in her hands anymore and it isn't in his holster again either.

"I cannot believe you told me your real name was Will the first time we met," Bristol says when we're still around the third floor.

"That was my baseline lie," he says, with difficulty.

Bristol reaches over and settles his collar where it got rumpled. "Well, it suits you."

We cross the lobby together, and Will behaves. He doesn't even look towards the front desk in a silent plea. I wonder what he's thinking; he's either too calm, or he's in shock. There are no sirens, even as we're out on the sidewalk again, the sun almost entirely gone. "I know a place we can get a car," Dolly says, taking out an ecigarette. "Prob'ly better to get our stuff and put this place behind us before we crash for the night and get some deprogramming done."

"I'm not—" Will says, and Bristol takes his arm.

"Hush, darling. There isn't anything to worry about right now."

"I wish I could believe that."

"If wishes were horses, then beggars could ride," I say.

Dolly huffs out a cloud of vapor laughing. "Bitsy, what?"

"Just an old saying."

Epilogue

After everything else, it really was only like six more hours in the car to get across the border to Mexico, and we do that before we get a hotel. The agency works globally, of course, but distance is always good.

Will is quiet for the drive, quiet in general. Probably thinking about his career, his family. It'll be interesting to see how the agency pursues this, if they want to recover or terminate. Maybe they already thought he was compromised; nobody ever said that outright in any of the files, but I think anybody who'd seen him and Bristol in the same room for any amount of time might have a sense of that. So, his supervisor definitely.

We get a suite in one of those all inclusive resort hotels that puts a wristband on you and makes it so easy to not leave, or at least not stray very far from its walls, beyond the kayaks they offer, the scuba adventure they'll take you on. Otherwise, lay out by the pool, and eat fresh chips and salsa daily and refill your daiquiris as needed, virgin or alcoholic. All of us speak Spanish, which make sense, but is nice to confirm.

Cortina from the other team messages me to congratulate me, hoping to keep the contact, I think. Which is fine, it's nice to have connections far and wide, at all levels. You never know when you're going to need somebody, and if you're smart, you never forget what it was like when you were just starting out.

Like Will is now, in fact. I'm pretty sure Bristol isn't going to let him far out of her sight for a while, but she'll have to eventually. Though also, the suite has enough beds for all of us, and everybody seems to have been sleeping in their own beds, so who knows. Dolly hasn't started making comments about it yet, which means it's serious.

www.ingramcontent.com/pod-product-compliance
Lightning Source LLC
Chambersburg PA
CBHW011230120626
46549CB00008B/3212